Everything Is Better In Pairs

Rebekah Lynn

Editor: Tori Smithers

Artwork by : Katiee Comer

Book Cover by Achleys Book Cover Designs

First edition 2026

Contents

Trigger warning list

This book explores themes of some heavy content, including but not limited to:

- Mention of Childhood sexual assault (not detailed)
- Trigger warning
- One night stand
- Parent's assault
- Sexual Assault (not between main characters)
- Blood
- Fighting
- Guns
- Death

- Stabbing

Please be mindful of these and other potential triggers. If you find any of these topics distressing, prioritize your well-being and seek support if needed. Your mental health matters.

Playlist

All I want By Kodaline

Fuck Being a Princess By Esme Rose

Dirty Thoughts By Chloe Adams

Do I Wanna Know? By Arctic Monkeys

I Put A Spell On You By Annie Lennox

Believer By Imagine Dragons

Legends Are Made By Sam Tinnesz

Grave By Chloe Adams

Lose Control By MEDUZA, Becky Hill, Goodboys

Earned It By The Weeknd

Love Me Like You Do By Ellie Goulding

Chicago Ice Vortex

ROSTER

Malachi Monroe, Captain, #33, Center

Micheal Monroe, Alternate, #22, Goalie

Luca Moretti, Alternate #11, Left Wing

Maverick Sinclair, #69, Center

Tyler Cross, #23, Right Wing

Jaxon Stevens, # 72, Center

Grayson Kline, #44, Defenseman

Ethan Summers, # 57, Right Wing

Derek Mitchell, # 88, Left Wing

Max McGrath, #77, Defenseman

Nikolai Petrov, #9 Center

Manin Carter #19, Goalie

Dylan West, # 17, Defenseman

Daryl Sims, # 1, Left Wing

Maxim Kovalev, #80, Right Wing

Owen Gallagher, # 27, Left Wing

Ryder Finnagan, # 30, Center
Carter McAllister, #12, Defense
Jared Brooks, #99, Right Wing
Finn O'Rourke, #4, Defense

Coaches
Head Coach: Logan Whitaker
Assistant Coach (Offense): Travis Caldwell
Assistant Coach (Defense): Ryan Holt
Goaltending Coach: Jake Vann
Strength & Conditioning Coach: Ethan Marks

For the ones who know that love doesn't always come singular

sometimes it comes in pairs,

strong enough to hold you steady,

and fierce enough to never let you fall.

Chapter 1

Julia

I wanted one night to be free from expectations, free from my last name. One night to just be a normal girl at the club. Not someone who is expected to be perfect or who gets begged to buy all the drinks because my family has money.

A voice cuts through my internal bitching, "Hey, beautiful, can I get you a drink?"

I look up from my empty glass and straight into the most beautiful pair of hazel eyes I have ever seen.

"Um... yeah. A whiskey would be great. Thanks," I replied.

He smiles, waves down the bartender, and orders two more whiskeys on the rocks. My night hasn't been great so far, but suddenly it feels like it might turn around.

"My name is Michael, but everyone just calls me Mikey." He offers his hand, and without thinking, I take it. His hand is bigger than mine... So much bigger than mine... So warm, and pale against my tan skin.

"I'm Julia." I smile, trying to hide the nervous stutter threatening in my voice. He's at least a foot taller than me, and solid muscles. His blonde hair is tied back, and you can see that the underside is shaved. There is a hint of stubble on his sharp jaw that I swear could cut diamonds. Those arms.. And don't get me started on his perfectly sculpted ass that fills out his jeans so well; it has me practically drooling.

He hands me my drink. "Thank you," I say, standing and heading back to the VIP lounge, where I've been alone all night because I don't feel like explaining why five men in suits are constantly hovering. Two outside the building, one near the dancefloor, one by the stairs, and the last one is stationed right inside my lounge. They are all massive and intimidating, and they are here because of who my father is.

Tonight, though. I want to be Julia. Just Julia.

"Do you want to come hang out with me?" I ask Mikey. "It's just me, so it won't be crazy. But you'd probably have to stay down here if you want... that." I give him a shy smile. I usually don't admit I'm alone, but technically I'm not. My dad always insists on the bodyguards, which is also why no one ever approaches me.

"Yeah, I'd love to hang out with you. Can't have you lonely in a club, can we?" He says, lifting one eyebrow in a cocky, devastating way.

We head up to the lounge and settle onto the velvet couches, and I catch him eyeing the guard by the stairs.

"Please ignore him," I say with a pathetic little smile.

Mikey nods, giving me space to keep talking. "So what brings you here all alone tonight, Mikey?" I ask, taking a sip of whiskey and letting my gaze travel over him again, this man's muscles alone can make a girl drop to her knees and worship him. I lick my lips and admire the view. I want to climb his ass like a spider monkey.

"I just wanted to grab a drink and hang out. The real question is, what brought *you* here alone?" He tips his head, studying me, like he is trying to get me to reveal every secret I am hiding.

"I am tired of all the expectations in my life, so I decided to come and be free tonight," I admit.

He nods slowly at me. "Well, free Julia... what can I do to make sure your one free night is even better?"

"I want a no-strings-attached kind of night," I say honestly. "Fun. With no worries, no insecurities, and no responsibilities, something I can look back on when life goes back to being... complicated."

That's the most honest thing I have said tonight. No strings attached is the perfect situation for me; no obligation, no knowing all the dark shadows that follow me everywhere. I have never been able to hold a relationship because my dad usually scares them off. But if I am being realistic, I am the daughter of the most notorious mafia don in Chicago; it's hard not to be scared of my dad.

Mikey steps forward, closes the distance, and puts his hand on my cheek. I look up at him. "No strings attached. I can do that for you." Then he bends down and kisses me.

The kiss starts sweet and slow, but quickly becomes powerful and needy. I grab his shirt and pull him closer. He grabs my ass and hoists me into the air. My legs automatically wrap around his waist, never taking my lips off his. I am drunk on his kiss. The world is spinning, and my body feels like I have been electrocuted. I am buzzing from the high of his kiss when I finally pull away.

"There is a bathroom down that hall to the left." I point to the hall behind me. One great thing about this club is that each VIP section has its own bathroom, so there's no waiting in line, and it's not entirely nasty. Mikey understands exactly what I needed. Keeping a firm grip on my ass, he put his lips back onto mine.

Once we reach the bathroom, I reach behind me to grab the door handle and open the door. When we hear the hinges squeak, Mikey kicks it open with his foot.

He scrunches my dress around my waist before setting me on the counter and spreading my legs wide. He gives me one more punishing kiss on my lips before he starts his trail down the column of my throat to my shoulder. He moves the strap of my dress down my shoulder and pulls down the cup of my bra, exposing my breast. He doesn't hesitate before his mouth is on me, sucking and nipping, sending white-hot pleasure through my body.

I fumble with his shirt and get frustrated when it won't come off fast enough. I groan while he continues to torture my nipples, causing my back to arch, and my ass almost falls off the counter. Finally, I grab Mikey's head and crush my lips to his. When the kiss breaks apart for a second, I yank his shirt over his head and throw it to the side. I have no idea where it landed, but I couldn't care less. I lean back and admire his body. Each cut of his abs and the little bit of hair on his happy trail leading to the deep V cut draws my eyes to the promised land. When I look up, I see Mikey's eyes darken with lust.

"Like what you see, princess?" He asks, his voice deep and husky. I lick my lips and nod, knowing my words would fail if I try to speak.

I reach for his pants, pop the button, and slowly lower the zipper. I try to push his pants down, but this angle I am at is not doing me any justice. I let out another frustrated groan and look up with my best puppy dog eyes.

"Mikey... can you please take off your pants for me?" I bat my eyes innocently, like I am not asking him to strip butt ass naked for me so I can touch every single part of him.

He pulls down his pants and boxers in one fluid motion, and holy hell, I am not prepared. The monster that springs free from his pants can't possibly be human! Is this man some alien half-breed? What the fuck did I get myself into?

My facial expression must have told him what my mouth didn't because I heard a deep chuckle, and I felt his lips brush my ear.

"You aren't going to back out now? Are you, princess?" My eyes widen, and I feel my cheeks turn hot with blush.

"No." I squeak out. Way to play it off, Julia... real sexy and smooth. Completely mesmerized by a cock that you squeak when you finally talk. He glances at me with a crooked grin and no care in the world.

"Don't worry, princess," he murmurs, " we'll go slow." I nod again because words apparently are not in my life anymore.

He runs his hands from my shoulders down to my hips, pulling me forward where my pussy is against his thick length. A shiver goes down my spine at the contact. I grab his cheeks and pull his face to mine.

"Mikey! If you don't fuck me with that monster cock soon, I might die!" I say to him with every ounce of seriousness I have in my body.

His laugh vibrates the whole bathroom as he runs his hand against my opening.

"Mmmm, so wet for me. No need to rush. I am all yours, princess."

He pushes into me slowly, and it feels like I am splitting open and stretched beyond anything I've ever known. I bite my lip hard to make sure I don't scream from the intrusion. He pulls out, leaving only the head in, and thrusts forward, inching further with each thrust.

"That's it, princess. You are taking me so well."

I groan in answer, the pain melting into delicious fullness as he sinks in completely. He waits while I adjust to his size, his forehead pressed to mine.

"Okay," I whisper. " You can move now."

He slowly starts to move, creating the most beautiful friction between us. The sensation is almost too much, but I am greedy and want more. So much more. I'll take everything Mikey is willing to give me for tonight.

"More..." the words come out in a breathless rush. "I need more, Mikey. Claim me."

He growls. Like an actual fucking growl, and quickens his pace. The sound of our bodies slapping together echoes, but I don't care who hears us.

It is just him and me.

Right here.

Right now.

I can feel my body climbing to the edge of ecstasy, and I know he's close too. His thrusts become more urgent, almost desperate.

"Mikey! I'm gonn..." I couldn't finish my sentence as I fell into the abyss of pleasure.

"Jules..." He stops thrusting. I can feel his body tighten in my arms, and then I feel his cum covering my walls.

Oh fuck. We forgot to use a condom.

Chapter 2

Mikey

Tonight ended up better than I ever expected. When Kai told me he had a date tonight, I was butthurt at first, then I said fuck it and went to the club to get a beer… Now here I am, stuck in my own head, completely gone over Julia's beauty. She's the kind of girl you see in your dreams but never believed actually existed. She has the most stunning, long, chocolate brown hair in loose curls down her back. Light brown eyes that are almost gold and pouty, plump red lips, I want to bite for hours.

She asked for one night to forget everything, and I gave her exactly that. But can I forget her? That is the real problem echoing in my head. I didn't want tonight to end, and I sure as hell didn't want to watch her get into that blacked-out SUV with the men in suits. Seriously… who needs that much security?

I pull out my phone and go to Facebook to look for Julia in Chicago. There are way too many. Why couldn't she magically pop up having a mutual friend or as a suggested friend? I lock my phone and shove it back into my pocket. Mom always said anything worth it won't come easy. Let's hope she's right.

I walk into my Condo, throw my keys into the key dish next to the door, and head straight for the fridge. Fuck, I am starving, and I need a beer to chase this numb feeling out of my chest. Why the fuck didn't I get her number? Oh, that's right... no strings attached. A one-night stand thing.

Fuck, this girl is going to be the death of me.

I crack open my beer and down half of it in one go, grab another out of the fridge, and kick the door shut. Screw food, I don't feel like cooking. I walk into the living room and flop down onto the couch. As soon as I turn on the TV, I see the same hazel eyes I have staring back at me from the loveseat next to the TV.

"Kai. Why the fuck do you have to always be a creeper?" My twin burst out laughing like he is the funniest person in the world. I roll my eyes and drink again.

"How was your date?" I ask, waiting for the details about the mystery woman he refuses to tell me about.

"Eh, she was ok. Kinda vanilla, if you know what I mean." He shrugs.

"Dude, we are identical twins. I know exactly what you mean. We share a brain cell most of the time."

"Speaking of sharing a brain, I can tell you are hiding something from me, Mikey. Spill. What the hell happened tonight?"

I want to tell him to fuck off and keep Julia to myself, but that's pointless. Kai and I don't hide things from each other. Never have. We shared a womb, clothes, a room, and a damn twin-sized bed for half of our lives. The therapist said we were codependent. He wasn't wrong, but he also couldn't fix it.

Kai is the yin to my yang, and it will stay that way until we die. I refuse to live in a world without my brother.

Our dad and mom used to fight over us being together all the time. One time, when we were seventeen, Dad got so angry that he slapped Mom and punched a hole in the wall. Kai and I both tackled his ass to the ground and made Mom leave the room. We told him that if he ever did that again to our mom, that would be the last thing he would do. He packed a bag that night, and we haven't seen him since. We don't know where he went. Don't care to.

Since that day, Mom hasn't been the same. She gave her all to Dad, and when he left without a goodbye, it left a daryl-shaped hole in Mom's heart. I feel bad that she is suffering, but I am grateful the fucker can't lay a hand on her anymore.

"Earth to Mikey!" Kai snaps his finger in front of my face. I shake my head out of my thoughts.

"Huh?"

"I asked what happened tonight. Did you at least get laid?" A shit-eating grin spreads across my face.

"Did I ever! Best fucking pussy of my life."

Kai raises a brow, "If it was that good, where is she? You didn't bring her home?" My brother is apparently firing shots because I can barely answer his question before the next one comes at me.

"Holy shit, man! Slow down." I hold up my hand. "I'll tell you everything after you tell me about your date. I have been asking about this date all week, and you haven't shared shit. So fucking spill the beans!" I come back with my shots. Fucker thinks he can hide behind me getting pussy. Dumb ass forgets I am him!

"Fine, how about this? You tell me about your night first, since your night was clearly better than mine, and then I'll explain my disaster."

I smirk. If his night was that shitty, maybe he deserves to know my dick had a better time than his did.

"Fine," I huff at him. "I went to Nocturn for a beer. There was this petite girl at the bar. She had long brown curls almost to her ass. I slid up next to her, got a good look, and holy shit, bro. That *face*. I would murder a motherfucker for a face like that." I can't help reliving it again, every detail of Julia burned into my brain.

"And? What else? You aren't this smitten over a girl you just looked at while at the bar. I know you better than that. Plus, she would be a fool not to go after you. I mean fuck! Look at us!" He gestures up and down his body, showing himself off like we don't look the exact same.

"Alright, alright. So I introduced myself and bought her a drink. She ordered a fucking whiskey on the rocks. A girl after my own heart!" I sigh, put my hand on my chest, and pretend to faint.

A pillow hits my head, and Kai laughs.

"But then she invited me up to her VIP lounge. One thing led to another, and we fucked in the VIP bathroom. She told me she wanted a one-night thing, a night to forget, all that good shit. So that's what I gave her." I pause and then remember, "Oh! And she told me I had a monster cock." I wink at him, finish my beer, and head to the fridge for another.

Chapter 3

Kai

A monster cock, really? I mean, my brother and I are above average, but I have never had someone outright call it a *monster cock.* And if they did, I'd probably pound them until they forgot their name.

"So... does mystery sex goddess have a name?" I raise a brow at him.

"Yup!" Mikey says from the kitchen, popping the P like a dramatic little shit he is.

"Grab me a beer, would ya?" He closes the fridge with his hip, holding up two beer bottles. Of course, he already knew. We always do. Our twin brains just work that way. This man is literally the other half of my brain.

"You gonna tell me her name?" I twist off the top and launch it at his head. He dodges it easily. Stupid goalie reflexes. That's one thing I don't have: his cat-like reflexes. The bastard can snatch a puck out of thin air so fast people blink and miss it. It makes him the best in the NHL, and I'm damn proud of him.

"Her name is Julia," he says. "But she was big on not knowing much about each other. She wanted a night without expectations or responsibilities."

Damn, sounds like she has a rough life and just wanted to let loose. It's too bad she only had one Monroe brother and not both.

Mikey looks up at me. "So tell me about your night with Emilee."

Fuck. Here we go. What do I say? She wanted to jump my bones the moment we got to the restaurant, and she mentioned that several times. Or maybe that she ate like a pig and ruined my will to live? Probably shouldn't open with that.

"Emilee was.... " Fuck what do I say? "Nice?" It comes out as a question more than anything else.

"Emilee was nice? That's it? You waited all week for this date, and all you say is that she is nice. Kai? What the fuck happened?" He looks at me with the same *don't bullshit me* look I give him. Fuck, I hate how we are the same person sometimes.

"Fine!" I groan. I take one more long chug of my beer before I have to spill my guts about the worst date I have ever been on. Dating trauma at its finest, ladies and gentlemen.

"To start, she was thirty minutes late. By then, I was so hungry I was ready to eat the goddamn table. And when she finally arrived? She talked about herself the entire time. And not in a cute way. I mean... I learned her dog has intestinal issues and shits all over her floor. Then she told me she has to shove pills up its ass." I pause and look at Mikey. His eyes are wide, and his mouth is hanging open.

"Right? I know," I say, holding up a hand. "I love dogs, man, but I don't need to hear about explosive diarrhea while I'm trying to eat. Then she chewed with her mouth open. Smacked her food. At one point, she started talking with a mouth full of whatever-the-fuck it was, and some of it fell into my water."

Mikey stares at me blankly, shell-shocked. I don't blame him. I was shocked, too, but I was actually the one there.

"Yeah," I nod grimly. "I was ready to walk out, but Mom told us always to finish a date. So I powered through. I paid the bill, walked her to her car, trying to be a decent human being, and then she climbed me like a spider monkey. She's barely five feet tall and was on me like a dog in heat." Mikey just continues to stare at me like I'm reading him scripture from a cursed Bible.

"It gets worse," I say. "My dick wasn't even a little hard. Not even curious. I just wanted to come home. She begged me to bring her home. And then she offered... everything. All three holes. A three-some. Sharing her. The works. And then..." I point a finger at him, emphasizing it. "She said I could cum in her."

Mikey chokes on his beer, spewing it all over our living room.

"Exactly. That's when I realized she probably wanted to get preg-nant so she could say her baby daddy is in the NHL. And look, you know I want kids. I'd have them now. But not like that. I want it to mean something, you know?"

He nods. We've had this conversation a lot. We're both ready, fuck he's been ready for years. Too bad he attracts women who are one step away from needing federal supervision.

"Holy shit, man. I'm sorry," he says.

I shrug. "It is what it is. I'm just glad you had a good time tonight. The way you talked about Julia? Sounded like wife material."

I mean that. I want that for him. A real woman. Not someone who tattoos "Property of 22" above her coochie and flashes it on national TV, yes, that happened, or someone who sleeps with a homeless dude and tries to pass off the baby as his.

"If she didn't say it was a one-night thing, I'd be all over her," Mikey admits. "But she had security with her. Like... real security. I counted at least five men in suits. So now I'm wondering what she needs that much protection from."

Hmm. That's different. Not many people show up to a club with full detail.

I stand, clap him on the back, and head for the kitchen to toss my bottle.

"Don't worry, bro. If she's the one, you'll cross paths again. But I'm heading to bed. Night."

"Okay, Yoda. Goodnight."

Chapter 4

Julia

"What do you have planned tonight, Jules?" My best friend Mel asks over the phone, way too upbeat for my sour-ass mood. I have been in a mind-funk ever since I met Mikey. I know it was my idea to make it no-strings-attached. I know it was me who wanted the one-night stand. I know, I know. This is all my fault.

But one month later, and I still can't get his stupid hazel eyes out of my head, and how he looked at me like I was the only thing holding him to this Earth. I was hoping I would be over this by now, but here I am, still fawning over a guy I can't have.

"Nothing. I am going to put on my baggiest clothes and curl up on the couch with a bottle of wine and Netflix." I sigh into the phone.

Mel groans dramatically. She's been trying to drag me out of the house all week.

One good thing about being the only child of a mafia don is that I don't have to work if I don't want to. I know that makes me sound like a spoiled brat, but if I wanted to do anything, I would run one of my dad's casinos. We own the majority of the casinos in Chicago anyway.

Mel clears her throat, and I realize I've drifted into my own head again.

"Huh? Sorry, I zoned out." I guess I should probably pay more attention to my phone call.

"I said," She practically yells, "get dressed in warm clothes, we're going to a Vortex game."

Oh great... A hockey game... Just what I need, freeze my tits off while watching grown men beat the shit out of each other.

"Thanks, babe, but no thanks. I'm staying in tonight." My hair is a mess, my mood's worse, and social interaction sounds like pure torture.

"Oh, I love how you think you have a choice. That's adorable. I wasn't asking." I can hear her smirk through the phone. "We're going out to the game. I got tickets on the board, and we are going. Doors open at five. So get your depressed ass up and get dressed. The Vortex is blue. So wear blue. Maybe you will find your future baby daddy on that ice!"

I groan as loudly as I can through the phone. "Fine! What time do I need to pick you up?" I am going to have a driver so we can drink. If I go to a hockey game, I am going to get a few beers to calm my nerves.

"Have the car here at four. I want drinks before warm-ups. I'm so excited!"

Of course she is.

We pull up to the arena and get in line. Mel is buzzing with energy, like she just snorted espresso, and I am the dark cloud that is about to rain on her parade. I am still not in a good mood. I don't want to be here, but she's my best friend and will do anything for her.

Once we scan our tickets, Mel pulls me to the spirit store through the crowd.

"You aren't wearing enough blue! We have to fix that." She pulls a hoodie off the rack and holds it up to me, tilting her head from side to side to see if it would look good on me.

"Hm, this will work." She throws my hoodie over her arm, grabs herself a beanie, and heads to the register. She throws the hoodie at me as soon as we step out of the spirit store.

"Put this on. You look like you wandered in from a fashion magazine instead of going to a hockey game."

"I don't look that out of place," I mutter. I didn't think I looked that bad. I am wearing black jeans, blue heels, a cute white top, and a black leather jacket... totally reasonable.

"What's wrong with my outfit?" I question Mel, who is in jeans, tennis shoes, a Vortex shirt, and a zip-up hoodie.

"Oh, nothing, Ms. Prim and Proper. God forbid you ever leave the house looking anything less than perfect." I roll my eyes. She steals half of my clothes anyway, so she has no room to talk.

"Okay, okay. Fine, fuck face. Let's get a beer and find our seats. If I'm being dragged out of my cave, I at least want to watch the sexy men stretch." A huge smile widens on Mel's face.

"There's my girl! Let's go!" She yells, pulling me towards the beer stand.

We navigate down the stairs to our seats with a beer in each hand. My feet are killing me, and I instantly regret my decision to wear heels, but here we are. I pull off my leather jacket and put on the hoodie Mel got me. It was a black hoodie with white, light blue, and hints of navy blue vortex in the center, with *Chicago* above the logo and *Ice Vortex* written on the bottom. It is super soft and has long sleeves to hide my hands. It's a weird quirk that I have. It used to make my mom mad, and she always complained about me stretching out my sweatshirts. This might just become my new favorite hoodie.

We hear commotion from the crowd, and when we turn to the right, we see the goalie come out in full pads, looking even bigger than I assume he already is. He has white and blue leg pads and a helmet with his Vortex Jersey on. The back says "Monroe" and "22" in big, light blue numbers.

The rest of the team pours out behind him. As Monroe goes to the goal, the rest start to skate around, shooting pucks into the net as they pass by. The goalie is blocking shots left and right. He is so fast that I barely have time to notice the puck coming towards him, and he is blocking it already. He is good!

“Mel! Do you see that goalie? He is good!”

“Yeah, Monroe’s one of the best in the NHL right now.”

Two guys skate to the side of the ice and start stretching. They have their stick on the ground and get on their hands and knees, pushing their knees out and back. Basically soft porn on ice, and I can’t take my eyes off them. I have never been to a hockey game, but I am starting to see the appeal.

They finish warm-ups and head back into the locker room as the Zamboni smooths out the ice for the game. We are playing the LA Guardians today. I don’t remember their team, and Mel keeps giving me shit about it. Her family is a huge hockey family. They have had season tickets her whole life, and she knows the players' stats and where they transferred from. It wouldn’t surprise me if she knew what they ate for dinner last night.

The players return to the ice and take their positions as the officials bring the puck to the center ice for the puck drop. As soon as the puck hits the ice, Vortex wins it. Number 33, Monroe…just like the goalie, passes the puck back to number 11, Moretti. He flies up the left side, weaving through orange jerseys with a stupid amount of agility.

Moretti passes the puck to number 23, Cross, who circles the net and passes it back to Monroe, who takes a quick shot.

The puck hits the back of the net, and the stadium explodes in cheers as the horn blares. The lights dim, and loud music plays.

In the next face-off, LA takes possession and rushes our goal. I see number 22 crouch down, and he follows the puck. Number 44, Kline, checks the Guardian player with the puck into the board in front of us. The boards shake. Neither of them flinch, recovering quickly and chasing after the puck.

Monroe takes the puck again, arcing down the ice. Teammates push through the wall of defenders trying to get open. LA's goalie drops into a butterfly, as Monroe winds up and fires. The puck rockets towards the top right corner, and the goalie catches it.

The whole stadium groans.

Monroe smacks his stick on the ice, skates to the bench, and hops over as number 69, Sinclair, skates out onto the ice, replacing him.

"So, are you having fun?" Mel yells through the noise of the crowd. I nod in reply to try to avoid a full conversation, given how much noise there is. I am going to lose my voice from screaming anyway, and the first period isn't even over yet.

Chapter 5

Kai

LA is bringing the heat tonight. The Guardians must have taken personal offense to breathing the same air as us, because these fuckers are going out of their way to piss me off. One more wrong move and I'm throwing my fucking gloves. Hell, I'm itching for it. A good fight always knocks the static out of my brain.

I squeeze water into my mouth and then jump over the board. As soon as my blades hit the ice, I'm off like a missile. I know I'm about to earn myself a penalty, but honestly? It's worth it. LA's too comfortable, and I don't like anyone getting comfortable unless I'm inside them.

I scan the ice. Moretti has the puck and is weaving through defense like he was born to make grown ass men cry. The crowd is roaring around me, the ground rumbles under me, and my blood feels fucking electric.

"AY! I'm open!" I bark at Luca.

This man is our honorary brother and permanent third wheel. Mikey and I are a package deal, but Luca comes with us, too. We have been playing hockey together since we were six and have made sure to be on every team together growing up. We share a brain cell when we're on the ice, there is no doubt about it. We told each other we would be in the NHL together, and here we are.

Luca taps the puck toward me, but dumb nuts, Harrison- number 5 for the Gladiators and one of their best defensemen- gets it from me.

Motherfucker.

Now, my blood is racing, and I am pushing my legs as fast as they will go to get the puck back. I'm seconds away from getting it when Protve- The six-foot-seven Russian giant– slams me into the boards so hard the plexiglass screams in protest. This man is a fucking tank. I feel my ribs strain against the glass.

I grit my teeth and turn, ready to elbow this fucking tank of a man right in the mouth. Then something catches my eye.

A flash of movement, then I see a set of warm honey-brown eyes.

I blink again, and there she still is, sitting in the front row. Curls down her back. Wearing a Vortex hoodie two sizes too big, with the sleeves covering her hands. She has black jeans hugging her thighs, and her mouth is slightly open in shock.

HOLY. FUCK.

She's fucking beautiful.

Not cute or hot or even sexy.

She is fucking beautiful.

She is the kind of girl you dream about, but never expect to see outside of your delusions. And here she is looking at me like she felt the hit I just took.

She genuinely looks worried… for me… The guy who literally fights people for a living.

Then something brutal and primal twists low in my stomach, and one word flashes in my head.

MINE.

The word hits me so fast, I almost miss it. I shake my head. What the fuck, Monroe? Get your head in the damn game.

I wink at her, because why not, and push off the board. I force myself back into the play before I skate over to her again like a fucking lunatic.

But shit… I already feel like one. I can't get her out of my head. Even while chasing the puck back into neutral ice. I'm still thinking about her. Those big golden eyes, the slight pink in her cheeks. Her lips wrapped around the end of her beer bottle… And oh, how those lips would look wrapped around my cock.

Fuck.

Focus.

We finish out the shift, and I hustle to the bench and rip off my gloves.

I spot Daniel, one of our physical trainers, and stomp towards him.

"Hey," I snap, grabbing his sleeve. "A girl. Brown curls. Black pants. Vortex hoodie. Golden brown eyes. Font row. Sitting with a blonde. You see her?"

Daniel blinks at me like I just asked him to solve world hunger. "Okay...? And?"

"Make sure she doesn't leave after the game."

He sputters, "Do I look like your bitch boy, Monroe?"

"You do now." I tighten my grip on him. "And if you don't? I'll tell every player in the locker room about your little underwear drawer secret." I don't actually know the details of the secret, but I overheard some of the guys in the locker room talking about it one day. I know if I needed to, I could get all of the juicy details from them.

His eyes bug out of his face, and he runs off to find security like his life depends on it. And if I'm being honest, it might.

I drop onto the bench, my chest heaving, not from exertion, but from something dangerously close to... anticipation.

What the hell is wrong with me?

I don't even know the girl's name, and I'm already plotting ways to keep her in this arena. I shouldn't care this much. Fuck I never care this much. I didn't care this much when I scored my first fucking NHL hat trick.

But that girl.... That girl has something in her eyes. Something soft. Something that makes me want to snap necks and offer her my jersey in the same breath.

I wipe my mouth with the back of my glove and lean forward, watching the play unfold on the ice, but my mind is nowhere near it.

The only thought on my mind is I need to see her again... NO scratch that. I will see her again.

And god help whatever stands in the way of that, because once I want something... Once a Monroe wants something... we don't let go... EVER.

Chapter 6

Julia

I swear I am in a fucking dream.

I would recognize those hazel eyes and that smile anywhere. They haunt my dreams every damn night. But there is absolutely no way I slept with an NHL player. No way. My mind is probably just short-circuiting.

There's one minute left of the third period, and we're up by one point. Monroe has the puck, cutting toward the Guardian's net like he's fueled by jet fuel and spit.

"Excuse me, ma'am," someone says from my right.

I tear my gaze away from Monroe and the puck. A security guard is staring directly at me.

"What can I help you with, sir?" I ask, smiling even though confusion is swarming through me.

"I was asked to escort you and your friend after the game." Escort us? What the fuck does he mean?

"Escort us? Escort us where?" Mel snaps beside me. I am glad I am not the only one thinking that.

"One of the players. Number 33, Mr. Malachi Monroe, asked me to bring you to the tunnel after the game."

My heart sinks. Malachi..Not Mikey...But those were Mikey's eyes. They had to be... This has to be a coincidence. A joke. Something stupid.

"Are you fucking serious?" Mel practically knocked me over to get next to the security guard.

"Yes, Ma'am. He said he wanted her," he nods towards me, "and her friend." So, Malachi specifically asked for me? What is even going on?

The buzzer sounds. The Vortex wins. The crowd erupts as we're guided up the stairs and through the maze of hallways. People stare as we pass, whispering like we're celebrities instead of two confused women with overpriced beer in their system.

I force myself not to snap at anyone. Last thing I need is my dad bailing me out of jail... again... I will never hear the fucking end of it.

We reach a set of stairs, and I curse myself for wearing heels. Note to self: no more heels at hockey games.

When we step into the tunnel, my breath leaves me.

I see Mikey standing there. Looking sexy as fuck in sweatpants and a Vortex hoodie. He is looking like every dream I refuse to admit out loud.

My heart is in my stomach, and my throat has a knot the size of a softball.

"Um... hi, Mikey. " My voice is barely above a whisper. He looks at me with such intensity that it makes my knees wobble.

"My name's not Mikey, little dove," he says with a choky smile, "but I can be your Mikey any night."

He winks at me, and Mel elbows me so hard I lose my breath

"Kai! What the fuck, man!" Someone shouts. "I told you to wait for me before leaving the lock..." The yelling stops mid-sentence, and I am met with the same hazel eyes I have been seeing in my dreams, locked onto mine.

"Julia? What the fuck are you doing here?"

He runs over, grabs me, and hugs me so tight he lifts me off the ground. My body remembers him instantly, and my lungs forget how to function properly.

"Ahhhhhh, this is the infamous Julia," Kai says from behind Mikey. I mean, I hope it's Mikey. I am so confused right now.

"Mikey?" I ask softly. Desperate for it to be him.

He cups my cheek, his thumb rubbing so gently it hurts. "Yeah, princess. It's me."

The breath I was holding for a month finally releases, and I hug him again. Clinging on just long enough to convince myself he's real, and right here.

I pull back and look at Mikey, then at Kai; it's the same face, the same laugh, and the same stupidly pretty mouth. I only see slight, minor differences, but it's almost impossible to tell them apart.

"If you are Mikey... then who is that not Mikey?" I point at Kai and raise my eyebrow in confusion.

They both laugh, and its the exact same sound, same timing. It's kind of creepy.

"Julia, this is my twin brother Malachi, but we call him Kai."

I reach out my hand to shake his. He catches it, twists it gently, and kisses my knuckles like he lives in a romance novel.

"Oh-kayyyy, so which one of you got checked into the board in front of me and then winked at me?" I cross my arms and tap my foot. Now I need to figure out which Monroe twin is which.

Mikey growls. Like, actually fucking growls.

"Seriously fucker? You were flirting with her on the ice? You saw her on the ice? What the fuck, man! Why didn't you tell me?"

Kai shrugs with no care in the world. "That would be me, little dove." Then he tilts his head towards Mikey. "And bro, I can't help it, we have the same taste. She is fucking gorgeous. I'm just jealous right now that you got to feel all of that without me."

He waves a hand, gesturing at me. The heat creeps up on my cheeks.

And what makes it worse… I glance around, and the entire team is standing there, witnessing every second of this.

"Ayyyy, Mikey got the pussy before Kai this time!" A tall, Italian guy yells, hugging the twins like he owns them.

"Oh my god," I mutter, covering my face with my hands.

"Luca, not fucking funny, man. This is Julia." Mikey says.

Luca's eyes go big in recognition, "The Julia?"

"Mhmmmm," Kia nods smugly and smirks at Mikey.

"Well, damn man. Good luck with that one," Luca says to Kai and slaps his shoulder as he walks away.

"Where are you guys going?" Kai calls, trailing after the group of hockey players now, completely ignoring Mikey and me.

I glance over at Mel, who is wide-eyed and watching everything with big eyes as if it were the best drama show on TV. I shoot daggers at her, and she smiles back at me.

"Hey, Mikey! You coming to celebrate the win?" Luca shouts, slinging his arm over Kai, and some other teammate I don't recognize.

"Yeah! Give me a sec!" Mikey yells back as the guys leave the exit.

Mikey turns to me, his eyes awed and wonder-filled. "Would you guys like to come celebrate our win with us?"

He sounds hopeful and possibly even nervous.

Mikey Monroe, NHL player, nervous?

I turn and lift an eyebrow at Mel in question.

"Fuck yes, we want to go!" Mel squeals, grabs my hand, and damn near runs out the exit. I catch Mikey's hand before Mel can completely drag me away from him.

We walk up to a lifted Chevy Silverado. Kai is in the driver's seat, smirking like trouble incarnated.

Mikey opens the passenger door and helps Mel into the truck, then opens the back door and helps me in before he gets in right next to me. He is sitting so close to me that our thighs touch.

I look at him. Looking at the face I dreamed about, even when I hated myself for it.

I lift my hand and run my fingers along his jaw, and his eyes soften instantly. He turns his face into my hand and looks at me with those earthy hazel eyes.

"So tell me, Mr. Hotshot," I murmur, "If Kai was the one who was flirting with me through the glass... where were you? I only saw one set of these beautiful eyes out there."

Kai snorts as Mel messes with the radio.

"Told you I was the better-looking twin!" Kai taunts Mikey playfully.

"We look exactly the same, dumb ass! How are you the better-looking twin?" Mikey shoots back. Kai just shrugs and starts tapping his fingers on the steering wheel to the beat of the music.

"Well, if we are twins, we must have the same last name. And I am pretty sure you saw two Monroes out there." He winks because he knows he is making me think this one through.

"WAIT!" I scream so loudly that Kai jumps, and the truck jerks slightly.

"You are the big-ass goalie?" My eyes go big as I am piecing together the puzzle.

The laughter from the whole car makes my cheeks burn with embarrassment. "Yes, princess," Mikey says, grinning. "I'm the big-ass goalie."

Then I remember warm-ups... Damn his ass during those stretches.

I lick my lips before I can stop myself.

Mikey rubs his thumb over my bottom lip as he puts his other fingers under my chin to make me look up at him.

"If you keep doing that, my tongue's going to replace yours." The heat in his eyes is so dark that it makes my whole body ignite.

"If you two start fucking in the back of the truck, just know I am joining in!" Kai calls from the front. I hear Mel laughing, but Kai's eyes in the mirror are dark and serious.

Butterflies explode in my stomach for a man I just met twenty minutes ago.

"Don't listen to him, Princess," Mikey murmurs as his hand cups my face and turns me to look at him again. "He's just jealous."

Without thinking, I lean forward and press my lips to his, fusing his lips with mine in one of the most electrifying kisses I have ever had. His tongue runs over the seam of my lips, and I open up for him. I grab his hair and deepen the kiss, fighting for dominance of the kiss.

When the truck stops, we break apart breathless.

Mikey looks at me and gives me his crooked grin that could ruin nations, and I pretend not to die inside.

I walk towards the bar, and Kai holds the door open for me. His hand brushes the small of my back, and my breath gets stuck in my throat.

I'm between the Monroe twins... And I feel the entire bar turn to stare.

"I wanted you since my face hit that board. Before I even knew you were the girl my brother is obsessed with, and now, little dove, I am obsessed, too." His voice drops. "Good thing my brother and I have shared everything our whole lives."

My brain flatlines... Shared everything?

Did he mean...?

Nope. Not going there. My face is already turning red, just from the thought.

They don't know who my family is. They don't know the danger. They don't know how fast my dad would ruin their lives just for standing near me.

And I can't let that happen.

My chest tightens as the air gets thin.

I need some space... some distance... fucking something.

"I'm going to the bathroom," I blurt out and bolt. I don't wait for a response or look back. Because if I look at either of them again... I know I won't run at all...

Chapter 7

Mikey

The second Julia bolts for the bathroom, my entire body goes tight.

Fuckkkk.. I knew it was too much for her. I felt her panic when Kai opened his stupid big mouth.

I take a step to follow her, then Kai's hand clamps around my arm. "Bro," He mutters. "We need to talk."

I jerk my arm out of his grip. "Not now."

"Yes, now," He snaps, stepping in front of me, blocking my way to Julia. "Because whatever the fuck is happening with her? It's not just you anymore."

My fist clenches at my side. "Back. The. Fuck. Up."

He doesn't... because of course he doesn't. Kai never backs up.

"You've been obsessed with her for weeks," he says low. "Talking in your sleep, staring at your phone even though she didn't have your number, fucking snapping at everyone. I wasn't born yesterday. I know you're in deep."

"And?" I grit out through my clenched teeth.

"And now I get it," he says, as his eyes flicker towards where she disappeared. "She's... fuck, Mikey. She's something else."

My jaw ticks. I don't like the way he says that, and I sure as fuck don't like the hungry look in his eyes.

"She's mine," I say without hesitation.

Kai lifts a brow. "Yours? Like the way the breakup chick last year was yours?"

My teeth grind so hard it hurts my jaw. "Don't compare Julia to anyone. Don't even fucking say her name."

And that's when I see a smirk ghost over his mouth. "So... it's real?"

"It's real," I spit. "I don't want your bullshit with her. I don't want you flirting with her. I don't want..." My words cut off.

"Us sharing her?" he finishes my words, way too casually.

My rage spikes to an all-time high. "She's not a fucking toy."

"I didn't say she was," he shoots back. "But you and I have shared everything our whole lives. Food, rooms, fights, women... everything."

"She's not one of those women," I growl.

Something dark flickers in his gaze. "Maybe not. But she looked at me, Mikey. You saw it. And she looked at you like she'd die if you stopped touching her."

My voice drops to a lethal tone. "If you're trying to piss me off, you're doing a great fucking job."

"Relax," Kai mutters, rolling his eyes. "I'm not trying to steal her."

"You better not."

He steps closer, chest to chest, voice dropping to a razor-edge whisper.

"But I am telling you this... whatever Julia is? Whoever she is? She's not normal. You saw it too."

I freeze, because he's right. There's something underneath her fear. It's something sharp and dangerous.

Something that is calling to every feral instinct Kai and I have.

Kai's expression goes serious. "You can pretend it doesn't matter, but something about her isn't adding up."

I shove past him. "I don't give a fuck. I'm going to find her."

"You think she's fine?" he calls after me. "She didn't look fine."

"She will be," I snap without even turning around to face him. "Because she's with me."

The music in the bar is loud, and people keep calling my name and reaching out to me for high-fives. Drinks are being shoved towards me, but I ignore them all because my mind is on one person, and one person only.

I look over to the hallway, the neon restroom sign staring back at me, and my pulse pounds in my ears. Before I can think, my feet start to move towards her. I don't remember the last time my nerves have been this bad... I also don't remember the last time a girl made me actually feel something.

Julia...

The last time I lost her, it was because I was a dumb ass and didn't ask for her number. If I lose her tonight, it will be because I was too stupid to read her panic.

I reach the bathroom door and lean against the wall next to it. I take a few deep, hard breaths to try to ground myself.

"Julia," I call out softly, as I knock once on the door. "Princess, are you okay?"

There is no answer, and my chest tightens.

I knock again, louder this time. "Jules... please talk to me."

More silence... Fuck it. I open the door an inch, making sure it's not enough to invade the privacy of the women inside, but enough so she can hear my voice.

"Julia?" My voice cracks this time.

And I hear a quiet sniff and a shaky breath.

"... Mikey?" My name is barely a whisper, and the sound fucking destroys me.

My mind is in overdrive now, and I don't give a fuck about the rules, signs, or anything else. I slip inside the bathroom and make sure no one else is in there. When the coast is clear, I lock the door.

When I turn back around, I see her standing at the sink, gripping the counter with her head down, and her shoulders are shaking.

"Hey," I whisper, stepping closer to her. "Princess..."

She tries to talk, but her breath catches, and she chokes out a sob instead.

"I'm sorry," she says, eyes still down towards the counter. "I just... I needed a second."

"You can have all the seconds you want," I reach out slowly to her, making sure not to spook her. "Just don't run from me."

She finally lifts her eyes, and I can see they are full of fear. Not fear of me, but something bigger, and I have a strong gut feeling she isn't going to tell me what it is either.

"I shouldn't be here," she whispers. "I shouldn't be with you... or Kai. I shouldn't..." Her voice trails off.

I cup her cheeks gently. "...Princess. Look at me."

She does, and she looks so broken and terrified, but also beautiful.

"You're safe," I tell her. "With me, you're always safe."

Her lip trembles as she shakes her head. "You can't say that. You don't know where I come from."

"That's the thing, princess. I don't care. I don't care if your dad is the pope or a cartel leader," I keep my voice firm, trying to get her to understand each of my words. "You're not going to scare me away."

Her eyes widen with a mixture of horror and disbelief, and I smile at her. I lean in, putting my forehead on hers.

"You could be dangerous as hell, and I'd still choose you."

Her breath hitches. "You shouldn't."

"Too late."

Her fingers clutch onto my hoodie like a lifeline, "Everyone I get close to gets hurt."

"Then stay close," I say, brushing my thumb across her cheek. "I can take a hit."

She lets out a broken laugh, "You really shouldn't want me."

"Too bad," I say simply. "I'm not going anywhere."

She leans in close and rests her head on my chest, and for the first time all night, her breath starts to steady.

I rub my hand over her head, and she melts into me like she's been waiting a month for this... and I secretly hope she has been because I have.

I kiss her hair and let her floral, earthy smell invade my senses. "I lost you once, princess. I'm not losing you again."

Her hands fist my shirt, as she looks up at me with tears still in her eyes.

"I don't want to lose you either," she whispers.

I smile into her hair. "You won't."

Because now that she's back in my arms? Nothing on this fucking earth is taking her away from me again.

Chapter 8

Kai

I'm leaning against the brick wall with my arms crossed, across from the bathroom. My jaw is clenched so tight it might crack.

I told myself I'd give Mikey five minutes. It's just enough time to calm her down and avoid me barging in and making things worse.

That was three minutes ago...

I don't hear any words at first, but I do hear a broken sob. My spine goes stiff... Something's wrong.

I push off the wall and move closer to the door. The music from the bar fades behind me as I hear Mikey's low, soothing voice.

"... Princess, look at me."

My stomach twists because he only uses that voice when he's in deep.

"You're safe... With me, you're always safe." His voice is protective and final.

Then I hear Julia's voice. It's barely there, but I can pick it out.

"You can't say that. You don't know where I come from."

I freeze. Not "I have a shitty ex" or "I'm scared of commitment."

No. This shit is deeper than that.

His voice continues, "That's the thing, Princess. I don't care. I don't care if your dad is the pope or a cartel leader, you're not going to scare me away."

Cartel. The fucking Cartel?

My hands curl into fists at my side.

I fucking knew it. I knew something about her didn't add up. What the fuck are we going to do? Get involved with a girl from the Cartel? That's a suicide mission at its fucking finest.

Julia's voice cracks again, and I turn my attention back to the conversation in the bathroom. "Everyone I get close to gets hurt."

I take a slow breath through my nose. My rage fills my bones. This isn't just some girl my brother hooked up with... she's trouble and fucking dangerous.

She's trauma wrapped up in soft skin and golden brown eyes. Causing a fucking vortex of whatever the fuck this connection is.

And Mikey... he's already drowning.

Then I hear the sound that seals my fate in this fucking mess.

"I don't want to lose you either." Her voice is small and broken.

Well fuck...

My vision starts to tunnel. I can hear the truth in her words. Hear the way she clings to him, and can hear the way she feels safe with him... something she probably hasn't had in a long damn time.

And what could be worse?

I hear myself wanting it too...

The jealousy hits me like a puck to the ribs. I hear fabric shift, and her breath hitch, and my chest fucking burns.

I shouldn't be listening, shouldn't want what he has, and sure as hell shouldn't feel the pull towards a girl who might get us both killed.

But yet here I stand... like gravity pulling me towards the door, and the bathroom goes quiet. The only sound I can hear is their breathing, and I finally take a step back. I need to walk away before I do something stupid, like rip the door off its fucking hinges.

When the door finally opens, Mikey steps out first, one hand resting on her back, like he is protecting her from the world.

All I can do is stand there and stare at her. She is clinging to my brother like he's the only oxygen left in the room.

Mikey notices me and narrows his eyes.

"Don't," he warns.

I lift my hands in surrender, even though my blood is boiling. "Relax. I'm not here to steal your girl."

His nostrils flare.

Julia looks between us, confused.

"Are you okay?" I ask her gently.

She nods, but I can tell it's a lie. I can see her fingers are still trembling.

"Let's get out of this hallway," Mikey says as he guides her past me.

But as she walks by, I lean in just enough for her to hear me, "Whatever you're scared of... we can handle it."

She freezes in her tracks, and her eyes snap up to mine.

She stares at me for a split second, I hear her breath stop, and I can see in her eyes that she believes me.

Kai Monroe–The fuck up, fighter, smart ass twin– just made her breath stop.

Mikey notices and glares at me. "This isn't a fucking competition," He grits out.

"It never was," I say quietly. "But she's not just yours."

His jaw tightens, and his hands ball into fists. He is ready to hit me.

Julia steps between us and looks from me to Mikey. "Please..." She whispers. "Not here."

We both shut up instantly. Neither of us can say no to her, and honestly, that should scare the shit out of us.

She turns and walks ahead of us toward the bar, and for once, Mikey and I are both silent.

But I know he can feel the shift in the air, and the truth hanging between us.

We are both in this now, we're both hers now.

And whoever she's running from? They're not taking her from either of us.

The second we step back into the main part of the bar, the noise hits me. The music is thumping, glasses clinking, and guys yelling over a pool table. The rest of the team is crowded around two high-top tables pushed together, already halfway through their drinks.

The moment they see Julia between us, everyone goes dead quiet for a half a second, then the chirping starts.

Luca whistles low. "Damn, she didn't run away from you two? Miracles do happen."

Cross elbows Sinclair in the ribs, and smiles. "Look at them. Twin guard dogs."

Sinclair nods like he is analyzing a fucking crime scene. "If one more person even looks at her wrong, Kai's gonna break a chair over someone's spine."

He's not wrong.

Mikey guides Julia to the table and pulls out her chair. He claims the seat to the right of her, so I take the seat on the left side, trapping her between us.

Her eyes flick between the two of us like she's not sure if she wants to scream, faint, or kiss us both.

Probably all three.

I can tell she is still rattled. Her hands are trembling as she reaches for her water. Mikey also notices and rubs his knee against hers under the table. Mine does the same a second later. I feel her stop trembling for a moment.

Cross leans forward with wide eyes. “So, Julia, is this like... a Snow White thing? But instead of the dwarfs, you get the Monroe twins?”

Mikey looks at him and shakes his head. “Cross, shut the fuck up.”

Luca laughs. “Bro, relax. She likes you. You’re glowing.”

“I’m not glowing,” Mikey snaps.

“Yeah, you are,” I say, sipping my beer. “You look like you got laid for the first time in your life.”

The table erupts in laughter and cheers.

Mikey rolls his eyes at me. “Fuck off.”

Julia blushes, but there is also a little spark in her eyes; embarrassed but amused. Good. Anything that isn’t fear is good.

Mel returns with shots, and I roll my eyes. Of course she does. She hands two to Julia.

“For courage,” she says with a wink.

Julia downs both shots like she’s trying to drown the entire last hour.

Mikey leans closer to her, “You don’t have to drink if you don’t want to.”

She looks up at him with mischief gleaming in her eyes. “Oh, I want to.”

I swear to god the growl that leaves my throat is involuntary.

Sinclair raises a brow at me. “Damn. Kai’s down bad.”

“I’m not down bad,” I mutter.

“Yes, you are,” Mikey fires back instantly.

The whole team turns and watches us like they're witnessing a car crash they can't look away from.

Julia drags her teeth across her bottom lip, a nervous habit maybe, but it sends a shock through both of us. Mikey's fingers tap on the table, and my jaw clenches.

When she notices, her cheeks flush, the tension ratchets up until even Luca looks uncomfortable.

He whistles and stands. "Alright, boys, I'm gonna go... talk to someone who won't end up as a homicide headline."

The team disperses slowly, leaving only the three of us in our bubble of heated silence.

Julia is the first to break the silence. "Are you guys okay?"

"No," Mikey says honestly, as her eyes lock on her.

"Not even close," I add.

She swallows hard, and her fingers twist in the hem of her hoodie.

"I didn't mean to make things weird."

"You didn't," Mikey says, turning towards her. "This is on us."

"And I don't regret a fucking second of it," I add, leaning in also.

She's panned between us, her cheeks flushed, and her breathing is fast. For the first time since she left the bathroom, she looks overwhelmed, but in a good way.

The front door opens with a loud bang, and a gust of cold air sweeps in.

Three men in suits walk in. They are clearly not normal clientele here.

I feel Julia go rigid beside us, as she stares at the men like she's seen a ghost.

Mikey stiffens, "Princess... who are they?"

The tallest one scans the room, with that trained eye you see Mafia men have in movies, and my veins ice over.

They are security, but not her security, from how scared she looks.

Julia whispers so low, you can barely hear her. "I need to leave. Now."

Mikey and I stand instantly, and every protective instinct I've ever had is screaming.

Whoever these fucking men are, they're not taking her.

Not from us, not tonight, not ever.

Chapter 9

Julia

The second the men enter the bar, everything in my mind freezes.

They scan the bar, not just looking, but hunting for me.

My lungs stop working, my vision tunnels, and the noise in the bar dissolves to just static from the blood rushing in my ears.

"Princess… who are they?" Mikey asks, his voice so low it's dangerous.

I swallow hard, but my mouth is dry. My heart is trying to crawl up my throat.

"That's… Reyes."

I point with a shaking hand at the tall one in the center, the one with the silver hair and the tattoo on his neck.

"Santino Reyes. My father's top enforcer."

Mikey stiffens.

I lift my eyes to the man on the right, with a shaved head, a broken nose, and heavy arms.

"Marco Cruz," I choke out. "He was my father's collector."

And finally, scar running from cheek to jaw, dead eyes, shoulders like a wall.

"And the last one is Luciano Vega. My father's… cleanup guy. Where bodies went after punishments."

My chest caves inward. I feel twelve years old again.

"They all used to work for my dad. They weren't just guards. They were violent. Sadistic. They did whatever he told them to."

My voice breaks.

"And if they're here? It means someone sent them. It means I was followed."

The three men keep looking around the room, and the longer I am in here, the sooner I will be found.

I look to Mikey, then to Kai, "I need to leave. Now."

They both get out of their chairs, and Kai steps in front of me without any hesitation, blocking their line of sight with his entire body. His broad shoulders and tense posture make him look like he is ready to take on an army… for me…

Mikey slides to the other side of me and grabs the back of my hoodie, anchoring me to him. They are protective and possessive right now. Both are wearing a terrifyingly calm expression on their face.

"Julia," Kai murmurs, never looking away from the men, "Look at me."

I don't look at him. I can't. My eyes are glued on the man in the middle… the one who dragged me out of my room by my hair when I was twelve for my "disobedience."

I choke on air.

"I need to leave," I say again, more stern this time. "Now."

Mikey doesn't ask any questions, just grabs my hand. "Come on."

Kai takes the other, and suddenly, we're moving through the bar so fast, everything blurs around me.

We pass the tables, the bar top, and Mel, who takes a look at our faces and doesn't ask a single thing.

"Kai, back door," she calls. "It jams. Kick hard."

We push through the swinging kitchen door. My senses are overpowered by the smell of grease and bleach, and it makes my lungs ache. My legs stumble, but the twins' hands keep me upright.

Mikey glances over his shoulder. "They're not following. Yet."

Yet... that word nearly makes me vomit.

Kai walks in front of us, reaching the back exit, and kicks the metal bar so hard the whole frame rattles. It sticks, as Mel said. He growls and kicks again. This time, the door slams open into the alley.

The cold air hits my face like a slap, and emotions flood me.

Mikey checks the alley first, making sure no one is waiting, then pushes me ahead of him and shields my back. His hand never leaves me.

"Kai, truck?" Mikey asks.

"Across the lot."

We move fast across the cracked pavement. My breath is ragged and coming out in pants. It looks like I am smoking with how cold the air is. My chest burns, and my legs are barely keeping up. Fuck these heels.

My fear rolls through my head.

You should've never believed you could start over.

The moment we reach Kai's truck, he yanks open the back door.

"Up," He commands. His tone is sharp and should frighten me, but it doesn't. At this moment, it actually steadies me.

I climb in with shaky hands, and Mikey gets in right beside me, sliding to the middle seat.

Kai slams the driver's door shut, locks everything, and fires the engine to life. The roar of it drowns out the sound of my heartbeat.

"Buckle," Kai says.

I fumble with my seatbelt, and then Mikey's hands are suddenly there, fastening the seatbelt for me. His fingers brush my hip, and I can feel the tremble in them.

Kai pulls out of the parking lot, tires squealing.

When the bar disappears behind us, I finally let out a broken and shaky exhale.

Mikey takes my hand and squeezes it hard. "Hey. You're okay. We've got you."

But he doesn't understand.

I'm not okay, not even close.

We continue down the road, and the truck gets warm, almost too warm. I'm not sure if it's the adrenaline or the twins. It might just be both.

Mikey hasn't let go of my hand. He's holding it like it's the only thing keeping him sane.

Kai's jaw is clenched, and his knuckles are white, holding the steering wheel. He hasn't said a single word since we left the bar, and the silence is suffocating.

The city lights blur past the window, streaks of neon and orange, as the panic races through me.

Finally, Mikey breaks the silence.

"Jules..." His voice is soft; you can hear the hurt in it. " Who were they?"

My throat closes as I stare down at our joined hands. His thumb is brushing slow circles over my skin.

I swallow.

"I used to know them," I whisper. "From... before."

Kai's voice cuts through the cab; it's lethal. "From your father." It's not a question, but a statement so direct it could cut someone.

I nod, barely, and Mikey's grip tightens like he wishes he could strangle the entire past out of existence.

"You tell me right now," Kai growls, "are you in danger?"

The question detonates something inside of me.

"I don't know," I breathe. "Everything was fine for months. Then tonight... seeing them..." My voice cracks. "It felt like being twelve again."

Mikey curses under his breath as Kai says nothing. And for a terrifying second, I think he's angry with me.

Mikey suddenly snaps his gaze towards me. "Where the fuck is your security detail?

I blink at him, startled by the venom in his tone.

"What?"

"You had five men with you at the club," His voice tight, "You had protection. Eyes everywhere. Why the hell were you at the game tonight with no one?"

"That's..." My throat feels tight again. "That's different."

"Different how?" Kai demands. "Because it sure looked like you needed them tonight."

My stomach twists, and shame burns under my ribs.

"I don't want to live like that anymore," I say quietly. "Always watched and controlled. I wanted a night without shadows following me."

Mikey exhales shakily. "Julia... That's slaughter waiting to happen."

Kai mutters a curse so low it vibrates through the whole truck.

"If I had it my way, I wouldn't let you walk from your bedroom to the damn kitchen without someone watching your ass."

Mikey shoots him a look, but doesn't argue.

I stare down at my hands. "I just want to feel normal," I whisper.

Mikey squeezes my fingers. "You're not normal to us. You're everything."

The words nearly undo me.

I look up at Kai and see his jaw flex, "They're not touching you. Ever."

Something twists in my chest, and I blink hard, staring out at the skyline. " Why do you care so much? We barely know each other."

Kai lets out a dark, humorless laugh. "Yeah. I noticed. Doesn't change shit."

Mikey turns my hand, intertwining our fingers together. "You don't get it yet, do you?"

"Get what?"

Kai glances at me through the mirror, his eyes burning into mine. "You're ours."

The words hit me like a punch to the gut, my breath stutters, and heat floods my neck.

I notice Mikey doesn't correct him; he just nods once. So slow and sure of himself. "Yeah. Ours."

My pulse trips. "That's... that's not..."

Kai cuts me off. "Argue later. Not now."

I open my mouth, ready to snap back, because how dare he say that to me, but then...

He reaches his hand back and rests it on my knee.

This is the first touch he's given me since the alley, and it causes my whole body to go still.

"We're taking you home," he mutters. "Where you're safe."

The way he says home makes my heart twist painfully... Mine? Or theirs?

I don't get a chance to ask, because suddenly we're pulling into the underground garage of the Monroe penthouse tower.

The truck slows to a stop, and everything goes quiet.

Chapter 10

Mikey

Kai locks the door behind us with more force than necessary, and when he turns, I see he is one breath away from breaking it off the hinges.

Julia stood in the middle of our living room with her arms wrapped around herself and her eyes fixed on some spot on the hardwood floor. Her shoulders are shaking, but she isn't crying.

"Princess," I whisper, stepping towards her slowly. "Hey... look at me."

She doesn't move. I can tell her mind is somewhere else entirely.

Kai moves first, circling around until he's in front of her. He crouches down, trying to catch her gaze.

"Julia."

Nothing.

My stomach twists. I've seen fear before; I'm a goalie. Guys charge at me at full speed every night. But I've never seen fear like this.

She looks like she is waiting for the nightmares from her past to walk through the front door.

I slide my hand under her chin and gently lift her to meet my eyes.

"Jules. You're safe."

Her breath stutters, but she finally meets my eyes. And that's when she breaks.

"They're my father's men."

Every muscle in my body locks up, and I can hear Kai freeze mid-breath.

Julia's voice trembles. "I didn't expect them there. I didn't think they'd be watching... not tonight. Not when I was..." She chokes on her words as her hand begins to shake. "Not when I was with you."

Fuck. I can feel the rage ignite in my chest.

"They're always around Chicago," she continues weakly. "But they don't usually... Interfere. They just report to him, watch to make sure I'm... behaving."

Behaving.

Kai steps closer to her, "Did he hurt you?"

Silence

Her silence is the fucking answer.

I inhale sharply. "Julia... why didn't you tell us?"

Her eyes flashed up to me with exhaustion.

"With what time? At the bar?" She snaps at me, and then her eyes get big. "I'm sorry. It's because I didn't want to drag anyone else into his world... my world... especially not you two." She lets out another shaky breath. "You don't understand. My father doesn't just get mad... he destroys... Anyone who gets close to me becomes a target for him. And I'm trying to get away from him without starting a war."

Kai curses under his breath and drags a hand down his face.

"Jules," I say softly as I reach out for her hand, "you're getting away from him. I promise. But you're not doing it alone. Not anymore."

Tears spill over her lashes, and I wipe them with the pad of my thumb.

"I don't want him hurting either of you," she whispers. "Your Careers.. Your lives.. He could ruin everything."

"Let him fucking try," Kai snaps.

Julia flinches, and instantly Kai softens, stepping closer to her and brushing a tear away with his thumb.

"Not at you, little dove. Never at you."

Her shoulders shake harder, and I pull her gently into my chest. She collapses into me like she's been holding herself upright for years, and my arms wrap around her automatically. Kai presses against her back, bringing his hands up to rest protectively on her hips.

As she is sandwiched between us, she finally exhales deeply.

"We've got you," I murmur against her hair. "You're safe here with us."

Kai's voice comes from behind her in a low grumble, "No one touches what's ours."

I feel Julia stiffen at the word ours, but she doesn't try to get out of our embrace. She just leans in to us, her head on my chest and her back pressed to Kai, as if she needs both of us to stay upright.

I don't know how long we stay there, but eventually her trembling slows, and her breathing steadies. I feel her fingers curl into my hoodie.

"Do you want to tell us everything?" I ask quietly.

She hesitates, but finally nods.

Kai and I guide her to the couch, one on each side of her.

Her hands twist together in her lap, a nervous habit I noticed.

"My father wasn't always a monster," she begins softly. "But power changed him. And when I tried to push back.. He made sure I never did again."

My blood runs cold.

"Julia," I whisper, "what did he do to you?"

She looks up, her beautiful, broken, brave face, and finally lets the truth spill.

Chapter 11

Julia

The words sit in my throat like broken glass. But Mikey is looking at me like the truth won't scare him away. And Kai… Kai looks ready to kill a man for breathing wrong near me.

So I inhale and let it out.

"Like I said… My father wasn't always like this." My fingers tremble in my lap as I twist the edges of my hoodie. "He used to be strict, yeah, but not cruel or violent. Not the man everyone fears now."

Mikey shifts closer to me, so our knees are touching, and honestly, it helps steady me.

"When my mom died, something snapped in him. He lost whatever humanity he had left." I let a small, humorless laugh escape me. "And he decided he needed to tighten his grip on everything. The casinos, the city, and me."

Kai moves his hand to my thigh and gently squeezes and nods at me. "Keep going, we are right here with you," he murmurs.

I swallow and nod.

"When I was twelve, he started sending his men to 'correct' me. To make sure I didn't embarrass him." My voice cracks. "The man at the bar tonight, Reyes, dragged me out of a family meeting by my hair because I didn't say 'yes, sir' fast enough."

I can hear Mikey grinding his molars.

"That was the first time," I whisper. "After that... any mistake was an excuse for Reyes. Sitting wrong, talking wrong, laughing." My throat tightens. "Trying to leave the house without an escort."

Kai inhales sharply. "He hit you."

"Sometimes." I shrug, "Sometimes he would force himself on me. Said it 'taught discipline', sometimes he would let other people do it."

A tear slid down my cheek before I could stop it.

"I tried running away once when I was sixteen." I laugh softly, but even to my own ears it sounds hollow. "I didn't even make it two blocks. He had men watching every exit of the property."

Kai mutters something violent under his breath, but lets me continue.

"When I turned eighteen, my father loosened the leash. A little. Let me move into my own apartment on the condition that I still answer to him and Reyes. Still checked in. I still went to events and dinner, and still acted like his perfect little daughter."

My voice breaks. "But every time I disobeyed, even in the smallest way... something bad happened. A threat, a warning, a broken window. Anything to remind me that I still belonged to him, and he would send Reyes to punish me."

Mikey's hand finds mine without hesitation.

"Julia," he whispers. I can hear the anger in his voice that he is barely containing. "Why didn't you go to the police?"

I shake my head instantly. "You can't go to the police about someone like him. They either work for him or fear him. And if they don't..." My stomach twists. "He makes them disappear."

Heavy silence falls around the room.

Kai runs his thumb over the inside of my thigh, slow and steady. "So you've been living like this... Alone... In the same city as him?"

"Yes." I swallow hard. "I've been saving money to leave Chicago for good. I almost had enough, but I needed time, and I needed him to think I was compliant so he wouldn't notice."

Mikey's eyes close for a second, like the thought physically hurts him.

"And tonight," I finish quietly, "when I saw those men... I realized he might already know I'm planning something. That's why I panicked. Because if he thinks I'm pulling away... if he thinks someone else has influence over me... he is going to go straight for them."

My breath catches. "And now he is going to come after you two."

Mikey's fingers tighten around mine immediately, "Let him. I'm not afraid of him."

Kai leans forward, eyes dark and steady. "You're not alone anymore, little dove. Not even for one second of your life, ever again."

Terror rips through my chest. "I don't want him ruining your careers," I whisper. "Your lives."

Kai shakes his head slowly. "He'd have to survive us first."

Mikey nods, sliding an arm around my shoulders and pulling me against him.

"And I'm not letting you go," he murmurs. "Not back to him. Not back to the fear. You are staying here tonight."

My heart stutters. "Here?"

"With us," Kai says simply.

My lips part, but I can't get any sound to come out.

"We'll keep you safe," Mikey whispers, brushing a tear from my cheek. "You don't have to run anymore."

And for the first time in years, the weight in my chest loosens just a little bit. Just enough to breathe... to hope...

Chapter 12

Kai

Julia is sitting between us on the couch. She looks so small when she is shaken and she is trying so damn hard to hold herself together.

But once Mikey pulls her into his side and her breath trembles against his chest, something in me detonates.

MINE.

The word hits me like a gunshot to the chest.

This isn't the ownership in the sense of her father. But in the protective sense. I'll burn the fucking city down before anyone touches her again.

She looks up at me, her eyes still red from crying, her lips parted. I can tell she is still trying to hide the unshed tears.

And right then and there, I'm completely gone for her.

I move before I think.

Before Mikey can say her name, I'm already in front of her, gripping her chin between my fingers, tilting her face up to mine.

"You're safe here," I try to tell her in a low, rough voice. But it comes out sounding like something completely different. It sounds like a vow.

Her breath hitches, and her gaze flicks to my mouth.

She wants me. I can feel it. Even shaking and exhausted... She wants me.

I feel Mikey's eyes on us, but he doesn't stop me. He leans back and watches, letting me take the lead like he always does when I get like this.

"Julia," I murmur, brushing my thumb across her lower lip. "Look at me."

She does, instantly.

God, she's so obedient, and she doesn't even realize it.

Not because she is weak, but because she trusts me. And that's even worse. It makes my chest ache.

"I wasn't lying earlier," I say. "You're not spending tonight alone."

She swallows, and I watch her throat bob. "Okay."

But that's not enough for me. Not right now.

I slide my hand to the back of her neck, guiding her forwards until her knees press together and her breath fans across my collarbone.

"You said you don't want him ruining our lives," I whisper into her ear. "You think you're a burden?"

She stiffens to my words, and I tighten my grip.

"Let me be very clear for you, little dove," I growl. "You are not a burden. You're ours."

Her breath stops completely, and the air in the room thickens.

"Ours?" she whispers.

Mikey's voice comes from the couch, low with desire. "Yes."

I feel her shiver, and she tries to speak, but her voice comes out soft and shy. “Then... show me.”

Those three fucking words end me.

I pull her into my lap in one motion, fast enough that she gasps.

Her thighs fall over mine, as her hands land on my shoulders. I feel her body melting against me, like she was always meant to fit here.

Mikey sits forward, putting his elbows on his knees. His eyes darken as he watches her perch on top of me.

“Easy, baby,” He says, nice and slow. “Let him take care of you.”

I drag my nose along her jaw and breathe her in.

She smells like fear fading into want.

“Tell me no,” I murmur against her skin. It’s the last chance I’ll give her.

She doesn't hesitate as she tilts her head for me, offering me her throat.

“Don’t stop,” she whispers.

A low sound tears out of me. It's feral and something I've never let anyone hear. I press my mouth to her neck, kissing and claiming her.

She arches against me, and a breathless sound escapes her lips.

Mikey swears under his breath and shifts forward. It’s like he physically can’t sit back anymore.

I slide my hands down her waist and grip her hips, guiding her slowly up the length of my hard cock. I don’t thrust into her; I just want to teach her the shape of my want for her.

She exhales shakily, “Kai...”

“Good girl,” I whisper into her skin. “Say my name like that again.”

“Kai.”

Her voice breaks, and I feel it everywhere.

I lower my forehead to hers and hold her in place with my fist in her hair as Mikey leans in behind her, his chest brushing her back.

He brings his lips near her ear. “You feel what you do to us?” His palm slides over her thighs in slow, torturous strokes. “This is what happens when you let yourself be ours.”

I feel Julia tremble between us.

I whisper the words that seal it for all three of us. “You’re staying here tonight, in our bed. With us.”

She doesn't argue, just breathes out one word. “Okay.”

And just like that... She’s ours.

Chapter 13

Julia

As soon as the words leave my mouth, Kai leans in and claims my lips. There is so much determination and passion in this kiss that it makes me dizzy.

"Kai. Please." I stumble over my words, completely breathless.

"Please, what little dove?" he mumbles over my lips.

"I need more."

My voice is barely louder than a whisper. My hips start to grind down on him and push my ass back on Mikey. I feel both of their growing lengths digging into me. Heat starts to grow low in my belly. I want them both. Right now.

Mikey's hands tighten around my waist as his fingers dig in. My breath hitches. His chest rises behind me; you can tell he is trying to control his breathing, but the tension in him vibrates.

Kai's eyes darken instantly. "Careful," he warns softly. "You don't get to ask for 'more' without telling us exactly what you want."

His hands slide up my thigh and stop just before he is where I need him. He hovers there, making me ache and wanting for everything.

"Use your words, Princess," Mikey murmurs against the back of my neck, his lips brushing my skin. "Or we stop." His words make a shiver run through me.

Kai tilts my chin, forcing my eyes back to his. "Tell us. Tell us what you need."

My lips part, but no sound comes out. My body is too strung up with need, and the weight of both of them pressed to me is burning me alive.

"I-I want you," I breathe. "Both of you. Now."

Mikey curses against my shoulder, and Kai starts to smile the slow and wicked smile that tells me he is getting exactly what he wants.

"There she is," he says, lower than I have ever heard it. It sends pleasure running through me. "Our brave little dove."

He kisses me again, but it's deeper this time, like he can't kiss me hard enough. Mikey's hand slides around my front and pulls me in tight, refusing to let me escape.

I am so wrapped up in them and wanted by them; it's euphoric.

And for the first time in my life, I don't feel afraid of being trapped.

Right now, I just feel chosen.

Kai breaks the kiss first, resting his forehead against mine as his breath shakes. "Ohhhh, big bad hockey player is out of breath because of little ol' me?"

"We're not rushing you," he whispers. "Not tonight."

Mikey turns my face towards him and presses a slow kiss to my temple. "You've been through enough, Julia. You deserve to be touched right. Wanted instead of demanded."

Kai's hand slips behind my neck, "When you're ready... We'll take care of everything you're asking for."

I swallow hard as my chest rises in fast, uneven breaths. "I'm ready," I whisper.

Mikey's arms tighten around me. "We know, princess."

He starts to kiss up my jaw, "but tonight… we're taking our time."

These men are saying all the right things, and I don't know how to process it. It's like my brain is glitching.

Kai brushes his thumb over my lip, "Consider this the beginning."

The heat between us three is electric, and I can feel the tension running so thin it's dangerously close to snapping.

Mikey pulls me back against him, his lips are at my ear as he murmurs, "We're not letting you run anymore."

Kai smirks and slides his hand up my spine. "And we're nowhere near finished with you."

The promises in their voices make my whole body shiver.

Mikey stands up and scoops me into his arms bridal style and starts to walk towards the bedroom. I look over his shoulder, and Kai is right behind us, his signature mischievous grin on his face.

As we walk, one thing becomes very, very clear to me. I'm not escaping these men. I have been claimed.

When we make it into a bedroom, I look around. There is a king-size bed in the center, a black-and-red comforter, red curtains next to a floor-to-ceiling window, and a black, oversized chair in the corner. Across from the bed are two doors, which I assume are the bathroom and the closet.

Mikey walks up to the bed and sets me down gently, like I am a porcelain doll.

I look up at him, hunger and pleading in my eyes. I want these men right now, but for some reason, they want to take things slow. I don't want to go slow; I want them now.

"I swear to god, if you two don't get your asses over here and fix the problem between my legs that you caused, I will handle it myself, and you won't even be allowed to watch," I demand, knowing if I don't put my foot down, these two will twinkle toes around me because of what happened, and try to bubble wrap me.

I look from Mikey to Kai. Mikey is standing there, just staring at me in disbelief that I just said that. Kai, on the other hand, is ripping his clothes off like it's an Olympic sport.

I smile in victory and reach for the button on my pants, slowly unbuttoning them and sliding them down my legs.

As soon as I catch Mikey's eye, he smiles and starts to take off his clothes, too, but looking slightly nervous.

"What are you nervous about, hotshot?" I taunt.

"I'm not nervous." He huffs out, and I laugh. I turn and look back at Kai, who is looking at me like I am his next meal. Little does he know, I will gladly be his breakfast, lunch, and dinner.

I see some silent exchange between the twins happen, and the next thing I know, Kai is on my mouth, devouring every sound that comes out of me. I feel Mikey's fingers running up my thighs, and slide between my pussy lips, pressing against my clit.

I grab onto the back of Kai's neck and tangle my fingers in his long hair, and pull his face from mine.

"If you two don't fuck me right now..." My words die off, but I know he got the hint.

"Yes, ma'am, boss lady," Kai replies and lifts himself.

I look down at Mikey, who is leaning back on his heels, watching my every move.

"So, princess. Tell us what you want." My thoughts go silent.

"Uhhh... I... Uh." Mikey and Kai both laugh at me as my brain completely glitches out.

"Don't get quiet on us now, little dove. You run this show." My breath catches in my throat. I'm in charge? What the fuck does that even mean?

"Oh, no, I'm not in charge," I shake my head.

Mikey grabs me by the chin and lifts my face so I am looking directly at him. "You are in charge. You will tell us what you want to do and how fast you want to go. If you want just one of us at a time, or if you want us to take you together." My eyes go wide at all of the power he is handing me. I am not used to having power; usually, that is taken away from me.

"So tell us, how can we serve you?" I raise my eyebrow at that. He just made this sound like I am a Dom and they are my subs. I have never actually participated in that lifestyle, but I have read enough smut to know some stuff.

I stand from the bed, thinking of what I want to do. I know I need this more than anyone realizes. To just shut off my emotions and feel these men inside me, with no other thoughts in my head. "Okay, if I am in charge… I want to try something new." Both men look at me and raise an eyebrow.

"Kai, lie down on the bed," I demand, pointing my finger at the bed.

"I have never done this before, so be gentle." I turn and look at Mikey, who raises a brow in confusion.

I climb back up on the bed and straddle Kai. He looks at me with hunger in his eyes.

I grab his monster cock and give it a couple of strokes, questioning my life decisions. Can I really fit both of these men's cocks in me? We are about to find out.

I guide him to my entrance and slowly lower myself on his length. Once I am fully seated, he groans. I lean forward and kiss him before I turn and look at Mikey.

"Alright, your turn." I stay leaning against Kai to give Mikey my ass.

You can see when what I am saying starts to click in his head. "Wait! You want me to fuck your ass?"

"Well, you can fuck my ass, or join your brother." I raise my brow to challenge him.

"As much as I would love to take your pretty pussy with my brother, I think we should prep you better for that one." I smile at him and just wait.

"Well, if you aren't going to join, I guess I'll just ride your brother." I roll my eyes and hear Mikey get on the bed behind me. He leans over and opens the bedside drawer, pulling out a bottle of lube.

The sound of the cap snaps through the air, and then cold liquid slides down my ass cheek. I wiggle a little bit and then feel Mikey's finger catch the drip and rub it over my tight ring. He slowly slips his middle finger into the first knuckle, and a groan leaves my mouth.

He slowly pumps his finger in and out of my hole, before he adds a second one, moving and stretching me, and fuck it feels so good. I push back onto this finger, making him go faster.

"Slow down, princess. I got you." Mikey whispers in my ear.

I look down at Kai, who is just watching me with his hands behind his head like I am the best show on TV.

I smile down at Kai, and then I feel it: Mikey's thick cock nudging at my entrance.

"I need you to relax, princess." I take a deep breath in, and as soon as I exhale, he breaches the surface.

It burns, oh fuck it burns. I have done anal, but never two men at once.

Mikey pushes in another inch, and I can feel my body adjusting to his size.

"Oh my god." The moan leaves my mouth before I can stop it.

Mikey finally pushes in all the way until his hips are flush with my ass. He pauses, "Holy shit, I have never been this full before." My breathing is already labored.

"Let us know when you are ready, little dove." Kai looks at me.

"I'm ready." I pant out, and my men start to move in unison.

The sensation of having both of these men in me is overwhelming.

"I need you harder." I whimper out. Neither of the men replies. Mikey just picks up his pace, and Kai follows suit. Oh fuck, this feels so good.

I feel my pressure start to build in my stomach. "Oh fuck, I am about to cum!" I yell out. As soon as I feel myself start to fall over the edge, I feel Kai and Mikey both tense and freeze. Then they completely fill me with their seed.

I lean down and kiss Kai, putting every ounce of passion into that kiss. I want him to feel how much he means to me. Even after just knowing them for a little while, I feel safe and wanted with them.

Kai reaches down and touches my stomach. "You are about to be pregnant with my baby."

"You got a breeding kink I don't know about, Monroe?" I question.

"With you? Absolutely." He gives me his panty-dropping smile.

"I have to agree with my brother," Mikey whispers in my ear.

I turn my head and kiss him, before I lift off Kai and fall to the bed.

Chapter 14

Mikey

I am lying here, watching Julia's chest rise and fall. She is peaceful in a way that I have never seen her.

I know I need to go to sleep. We have practice at six in the goddamn morning. Coach will skate our asses raw if we show up half-dead.

But I can't seem to close my eyes. Every time she twitches... or her breath hitches... I feel it in my chest. She is reliving those nightmares from her past all over again.

And I won't lie. I feel like if I look away for too long... she might vanish.

Kai is on the other side of her, one arm thrown over her waist like he's claiming his territory even in his sleep. He is in a deep sleep, also, the kind he only gets when he feels safe. But even when he is unconscious, his grip on her is protective and possessive.

Julia shifts, turning slightly towards me. A small sound leaves her throat, something between a whimper and a sigh. Then her brows pull together like something in her dream is hurting her.

I brush my knuckles along her cheek, making sure to be careful as hell not to wake her. The soft, gentle touch has her face relax instantly.

Jesus.

She doesn't even know what that does to me.

Her lips part, and she nuzzles into my palm. It's like she does it on instinct, like she's been doing it for years.

I lean in without thinking and press a soft kiss to her temple. Whispering in her ear, "I've got you, princess."

And I do... God help me, I do.

She breathes out a warm, shaky breath that lands straight to my heart, and she relaxes.

I should sleep... I should turn off the part of my brain that's wired to her every move. But instead, I lie here memorizing the way the moonlight hits her cheekbone, the faint shadow of her lashes, and the tiny scar above her eyebrow.

Kai shifts behind her, pulling her closer to his chest. She fits between us like she was made to belong right here.

And maybe... she was.

I exhale slowly and force my eyes to close, but only for a moment.

For this split moment, I can pretend that she is ours forever, and tomorrow she won't be gone when we get home from practice.

Chapter 15

Julia

Something loud and angry drags me out of sleep.

BEEP. BEEP. BEEP.

No... no, this can't be real. Who in their right mind sets an alarm for—

A hand slams into the nightstand, and then I hear Kai groan; his voice is thick and rough with sleep. “Fuck off.”

I blink awake and instantly realize I’m trapped.

I take in my surroundings from my pinned spot.

There is a warm, hard breath on my neck. A heavy arm banded across my waist, and a wild thump-thump-thump of someone’s heartbeat pressed against my back.

Mikey.

Then another body on my front, chest to chest, with a leg thrown over mine.

Kai.

I am sandwiched.

My entire body is overheating because I'm very aware that both of them sleep shirtless. And apparently… They are clingy.

Kai's eyes crack open first, "Well," his deep voice rumbles, vibrating through my bones. "Morning, little dove."

His hand flexes on my thigh, and my breath stutters.

Behind me, Mikey shifts, pulling me tighter against his chest with a soft, sleepy groan. His lips brush the back of my shoulder, which lights a fuse straight down my spine.

"Mmmm… Jules…" He murmurs, half-asleep. "Warm…"

I swear my soul leaves my body at his groggy words.

"Kai," I whisper, because he's awake more than Mikey, "you have practice?"

"Uh-huh," He says, unbothered as he starts to trace slow circles on my thigh, slowly drifting higher… then higher… too high…

My stomach drops. Heat blooming low and fast in my belly.

"Mikey," I try next.

He tightens his arm around me, pulling me flush against all of him.

I feel every inch of him. Every muscle and hard, sleepy line of him.

"Five more minutes," he mumbles into my neck. Then presses a soft kiss against my skin.

I jolt, and Kai's eyes snap to me. The look of possessive protection flickers across his face.

"Easy," he says, leaning closer, letting his warm breath ghost across my lips. "You okay?"

No... Not even a little. My pulse is pounding, and my brain is mush as electricity flows through my system.

"Y-yes," I manage to squeak out.

"You sure?" He brushes his nose against mine. "Because you sound like you need something."

My body ignites like an inferno.

"Kai," I say as a warning.. Or maybe a plea.. At this point, I don't even know which.

Mikey lifts his head, hair a mess, and voice gravel-deep. "What's going on?"

Kai keeps his eyes locked on me, smirking. "Little dove's worked up."

I choke on my spit. "I... no... I'm not."

Mikey lifts up onto one elbow and looks at my face, then smirks also. "Yeah. You are."

The air in the room shifts as Kai leans in until his lips touch mine. "We should be getting ready for practice," he murmurs.

"Yes," I whisper.

"Should," Mikey echoes behind me as his fingertips brush up my hips.

No one moves for a tense moment.

Kai lifts his hand and cups my jaw, and Mikey's fingers slide to my waist. And just like that... I'm caught, figuratively and literally, between two bodies, two stares. Two men who are barely holding back what they want.

My pulse is a drum, pounding through my body.

"Kai?" I whisper.

"Yeah, baby?"

I run my hand down his chest until I dip my hand into his sweat-pants and find his very hard cock with my hand. I give it a squeeze, and he lets out a groan.

I slide my hand up and down his length through his sweat pants, as I feel Mikey moving his hand down my body to my pussy, rubbing tight circles over my clit.

I let go of Kai and roll over to my back, reaching my hand to the waistband of both of their sweats and sliding my hand under. I grab onto both of their hard lengths and start to move my hand up and down their length.

Mikey starts to pick up his circles on my clit, and then I feel Kai's hand, his fingers at the entrance of my pussy. He thrusts me in one quick thrust and starts to pump his fingers in and out of me.

The sounds that leave my throat are not human at this point.

I pump up their shafts and gather the precum at the tip and swirl it around the head of their cocks using it as lube to keep up my pace.

A few more thrusts from Kai, and I am coming apart. As I cum I make sure to keep up my pace until Mikey and Kai both explode, making a complete mess of their sweatpants.

When we are all spent, I pull my hands out of their pants and turn my head to Mikey. I smile up at him and give him a quick kiss. Then turn and do the same for Kai.

"Now you two need to get up and go to practice before you get in trouble."

"For you? The trouble will be worth it." Mikey mutters, and Kai grunts in agreement.

Chapter 16

Kai

We're screwed.

The second Mikey and I walk into the rink, helmets in hand, the whole team turns to look at us. My skates are undone, and Mikey's gear is halfway on; both of us are breathing like we sprinted the entire way.

Some smirk, some raise brows, some just shake their heads like they're watching two idiots walking into their own execution.

And then there is coach...

Coach Whitaker looks like he crawled straight out of hell for the sole purpose of murdering us. He blows the whistle so hard I think a vein popped in his forehead.

"Monroe!" Both of our heads snap up like a reflex.

He stalks towards us with so much anger and force, he looks like a man who has waited his whole life to chew our asses.

"You two think practice starts whenever the hell you feel like rolling out of bed?"

I keep my face blank, and I can see Mikey in my peripheral vision already fighting a smirk.

Fucking Idiot.

"No, Sir," I say, making sure I sound firm.

Coach steps into my space. "Late."

"It's not.." Mikey starts.

Coach raises his hand to stop him. "Don't. Don't you dare give me an excuse. I don't want to hear it from either of you."

My jaw ticks, and Mikey looks up at the ceiling.

Coach points to the center ice. "Drop your gear. Lines. Both of you. Now."

Groans echo across the rink from the other players.

Coach turns, blows his whistle again, and shouts.

"THE WHOLE TEAM SKATES UNTIL THEY'RE DONE. MOVE!"

Eighteen sets of blades bite into the ice at once, every guy glaring daggers at us as they take off.

"Great," Luca mutters. "This is why we don't let the Monroe twins make decisions."

Mikey shrugs. "Could be worse. We could be your Captain and your Alter... OHHHH wait! We are!"

I lace up my skates and hit the ice hard. The cold burns straight through me as we both take off.

First set: fine.

Second set: Still fine.

By the tenth set, Mikey is wheezing, and I'm sweating like a whore in church. When we look over at the coach, he hasn't even blinked once.

"Pick it up, girls!" Coach screams, pacing the boards. "My grandmother skates faster than this!"

I flip him off mid-stride.

Coach blows the whistle again. "Twenty more!"

Mikey shoves my shoulder. "Stop pissing him off."

"Can't help it," I gasp. "Born this way."

By set... honestly, I've lost count... my legs are on fire. But the burning isn't the problem.

The problem is her... Julia... My Julia...

Every time I blink, I see her from this morning; Warm, flushed, and sandwiched between us like she belonged there. The way her breath felt against my mouth and her voice all soft and wretched when she whispered my name.

Christ.

Focus.

Hockey.

Skating.

Do not get a hard-on during lines.

Mikey elbows me when we turn. "Stop thinking about her."

"I'm not," I lie... badly, I might add.

"You are." He grins like the menace he is. "You look like you're trying not to combust. Or cum in your pants."

"Shut up and skate."

"Can't. Dying."

"Good."

Coach blows the whistle. I swear the man enjoys our suffering.

"Done!" he shouts. "Get back in line! You two, don't waste another second of my time, or I swear I'll..." Then coach stops mid-rant, looking over my shoulder. When I turn, I see Julia walking in.

She's standing at the edge of the rink in one of Mikey's hoodies... No, actually, my hoodies and leggings that should be fucking illegal. She's holding a coffee in each hand. Her cheeks are pink from the cold, and she looks like she has no idea the entire team is staring at her.

My lungs forget how to work, and Mikey slams straight into me because apparently, he forgot how to skate.

We both hit the board like idiots.

Coach turns slowly. Looks at her, then to us.

"Ohhh," he says. "Now it makes sense."

The team erupts into laughter, and I want to drown all of them.

Julia blinks, confused. "Um... hi?"

I skate over, ripping off my helmet. "You're not supposed to be walking around without security."

She smiles at me, "I'm in your rink. I think I'm safe."

Mikey joins us, leaning over her shoulder. "Is that coffee for us?"

She hands it to him.

Coach claps his hands. "Alright, Romeo and Romeo, quit flirting on my ice!"

Julia's cheeks flare bright red.

Mikey throws an arm around her shoulders. "Ignore him. He wasn't loved as a child."

"I HEARD THAT!"

We both smirk. Julia's eyes meet mine again, and everything inside of me settles.

Practice, the exhaustion from the lines, Coach screaming... none of that matters right now. Because she's here.

And for the first time in years, the rink doesn't feel like the only place I belong.

Chapter 17

Mikey

The locker room is full of tension. The guys are ripping off their pads and cursing under their breath because they are still pissed about the drills Kai and I dragged them into.

Whatever.

They'll get over it. I have done the same shit multiple times for them.

What I won't get over is the fact that I am still shaking, not from the lines, but from Julia waking up in our bed.

God, that girl. One taste of her, and I'm a goner.

I'm halfway through shoving my pads into my bag when the room shifts.

The energy feels like the oxygen is getting sucked straight out of the air.

I feel Kai go still beside me, and my twin-senses kick in immediately. Before he turns around or stiffens, I know we are no longer alone. I smell cologne. Not the shit our teammates wear, but the expensive, sharp shit that belongs in a boardroom.

I hear footsteps next; they are slow and confident, like someone who walks into dangerous places, knowing no one will stop him.

I turn, and my stomach drops straight to the floor.

A man in a freshly pressed charcoal suit is standing in the middle of our locker room, hands behind his back, like he is strolling through a store inspecting merchandise.

He shouldn't be here. No one looks like that in a hockey rink at eight in the morning.

No one belongs at this rink except us.

But this man? He belongs to another world entirely... a world I escaped at sixteen and promised myself I'd never return to.

He smiles when he sees me. It's an empty smile, but that is almost more frightening.

"Michael Monroe," He says smoothly, like he is greeting an old friend at a barbecue instead of standing in a room full of half-dressed, sweating athletes who could break his jaw in a single hit. "It's been a while."

I can feel my throat closing. It's a fucking chokehold. I feel like a vice tightening because I know him. I know exactly who he is. And every atom in my body is screaming to run, but my legs won't move.

Fuck. He shouldn't be here. Not this man, not from that world...

The whole team goes silent, West stops halfway while removing the tape from his wrist, and fucking Luca drops a skate. He knows what world this man comes from. He is from this world as much as we are.

Coach steps out of his office and freezes.

The man pays none of them attention, his eyes locked on me.

"We had hoped," he continues, hand still calmly folded behind him, "you would reach out before now."

My pulse spikes up, and Kai steps closer to me. He is trying to protect me, but I subtly angle my body to block him from the man's line of sight.

Kai can't be involved. He can't. He got out clean.

I didn't.

The man tilts his head slightly, eyes flicking over my shoulder towards Kai. And just like that, his message is crystal clear.

They know everything; they know where we are, they know who we are with, and they know who we are protecting.

He steps closer, his Stefano Ricci's silent on the concrete, until he is an arm's reach away.

I hold my ground, but just barely.

"You were asked," he said softly, "to remember the favor you owe."

I swallow hard and keep my voice low. "What do you want?"

His smile widens like a predator that is about to catch its prey.

"Your debt is being called in."

I feel Kai tense behind me, ready to lunge and rip this man in half with his bare fucking knuckles.

I shoot my arm back, stopping him.

He shouldn't be dragged into this. Not because of me.

The man speaks again, voice almost gentle. "We'll meet tonight. Midnight. I'll text you the address."

He turns to leave, but pauses at the doorway and looks at me. Then mutters the words I feared more than anything. "She looks very much like her mother."

A chill rips down my spine.

Julia.

They followed us, they saw.

Kai curses under his breath, but I can't even speak.

The man gives me one last thin smile. "Don't be late, Michael."

And just like that, he is gone, leaving the entire team frozen, horrified, and confused.

Kai is staring at me like I just went cold on him, and I am trying not to throw up.

Because of the past I buried? Just walked into my locker room in a custom fucking suit.

And Julia's danger? It's no longer a possibility... It's here.

Chapter 18

Kai

Julia practically sleepwalks into the penthouse the second we step through the door. She's still wearing my hoodie. She is practically drowning in it. Her eyes are half-closed, and her cheeks are flushed from exhaustion.

"Go take a nap, little dove," I whisper, brushing my hand over her spine.

She nods, saying something softly, then disappears into Mikey's room— her room now, whether she knows it or not. The door clicks shut behind her, and the apartment goes eerily quiet.

I watch Mikey pace the living room, back and forth. I want to tell him not to go. Shout it at him, but I know he won't listen. Ever since we left that life, he has been on edge, like he is waiting for the ghost of our pasts to come back and haunt us.

The burner phone we keep for emergencies buzzes. Mikey flips it open and reads the text. I am hovering over his shoulder to read it also.

Unknown:Midnight. 1783 Fifth. Don't be late.

I step back and look at Mikey, crossing my arms over my chest.

"So do you want to explain?" I know there is more to what is going on that he isn't telling me. And it's pissing me off. We don't do secrets.

Mikey sighs and flops down on the couch. Throwing his arm over his eyes, like he is overwhelmed.

"You remember when we were sixteen, and the guy forced himself on mom?" Well, I guess we are taking an unpleasant trip down memory lane.

I walk into my house after a long ass practice. Mikey told me to head home without him; he had to talk to the coach.

I throw my bag on the ground and head upstairs to shower. I fucking stink, and if I think I stink, Mom is for sure going to bitch about it.

Mikey and I are working our asses off trying to get seen by scouts early for the NHL. I know he is set. He is the best high school Goalie in the fucking country. And I know I'm a damn good center. I have been fucking captain since my freshman year. And man, did that piss off the seniors.

I walk into mine and Mikey's shared bathroom, flip the nozzle to Satan's ballsack hot, and start to strip my sweat suit. When I get in, the water soothes my skin, and I lean in, embracing the hot water on my aching muscles. Fucking James checked me into the board today so damn hard I saw stars. I know my ribs and shoulder are going to have bruises from that hit.

I finish cleaning up and get out of the shower, getting dressed in my faded blue jeans and my Linkin Park band tee. Now, snack time. I don't know how Mom keeps food in this house. I swear, Mikey and I are always hungry, and we eat a fuck ton.

Speaking of mom, I wonder where she is. Her car is in the driveway.

"MOM!" I yell through the house.

I get no answer, but I hear something coming from her room. That's weird... She usually will reply, even if she is showering or doing something.

I walk up to her room and try to listen in. It's cracked, but I am nervous to look in. What if she is getting it on? But honestly, she still cries over dad leaving, so I doubt it. Six years, and she is still in love with the bastard.

I peek through the crack, and I see my mom's head lolling to the side, blood dripping down her face, and her eyes rolling to the back of her head.

I push the door open more, as quietly as I can, and I see a man, his pants around his thighs, slamming into my mom, as she lies there, broken and unaware.

I SEE RED.

I slam open the door so hard the handle sticks into the wall, and I charge the guy. I pull him off my mom and throw him across the room. His head hits the dresser, and he looks up at me, confused.

I grab him by the hair and slam his head into the dresser again, and then slam my fist into his face. I keep hitting him, waiting for him to do anything to fight back, but he just sits there.

I see his eyes roll to the back of his head, just like my mom's are, and I throw him on the ground. His pants are still down, and I kick him as hard as I can in the dick.

"You think you can force yourself on my mom? You think that because you have a dick, you can do what you want?" I am screaming at him.

I grab his hair again and slam it into the ground. "Well, let me make something very clear to you, ass wipe! This is my mom! And I will always protect my family."

I continue to punch him repeatedly until I feel hands on my shoulders pulling me back.

I elbow whoever is behind me, and then crawl back to the man on the ground, who is no longer recognizable.

"Kai. Stop. He's not moving." I hear Mikey's voice softly in the back of my head. Is he actually here, or is it a figment of my imagination?

The arms wrap around me again, but this time they are holding me so tight I can't move.

"Kai, I got you. Come back to me." I hear my brother. The only person in this world to bring me out of the red haze.

"Yeah, I remember," I reply, shaking the memory out of my head. Fuck that guy, he deserved what he got.

"Well, that guy worked for De Luca." My eyes go wide in recognition of the name.

"What do you mean, 'he worked for De Luca'" I ask. This mother fucker better not say what I think he is going to say.

I clench my fists at my side and wait for him to get the courage to say the words that he needs to.

"Well, the guy went to the hospital and died. So De Luca had a hit out for you. I made a deal with him that if he spared you, I would owe him a debt." Mikey isn't looking at me; you can see the shaking in his hands as he speaks.

This mother fucker just told me that he spared my life and is indebted to the fucking mafia! I thought we were out of this lifestyle.

"Michael, what the fuck do you mean you owe him a debt..." I blink at him, not sure what exactly to think.

"Exactly what it sounds like, Kai! I have to go tonight and pay my debt so we can be free. I didn't think this would happen. We did some stupid shit when we were sixteen, running errands for the fucking Mafia wasn't our best fucking move. And then you killed the dude, I had to do it to keep you safe."

His words are sinking into me, like a sick poison eating at my insides. I am trying not to blow up on him for keeping this from me for ten years.

Ten fucking years... why are they all of a sudden coming back for the favor after ten years?

"Okay, so you go tonight, they ask your favor, and what? You just do whatever they ask?" I know it sounds like a stupid question, but we got out of that lifestyle for a reason. We have morals now. Well, at least more than these fuckers do.

"Yeah, basically." He says with a loud sigh.

"And I'm guessing you won't let me go with you?" He replies with just a shake of his head.

"Are you at least going to carry when you go?" My questions are all over the place, like my thoughts. I can't lose my fucking brother. He is the other half of me. I will lose my fucking soul.

"Yes, I will grab my gun before I go. But I can guarantee they will strip me beforehand, and you need to stay here. Someone needs to stay with Julia. She needs to be in the dark about where I'm at tonight. I don't need her knowing I am meeting her father."

Wait a mother fucking minute. Her father? When the fuck did he piece that shit together?

"You are meeting Julia's father!" The question comes out more of a demand than a question, but still. What the fuck?

"Yes, I told you I looked her up. When I found pictures of her with him at Galas and events, I pieced it together. But it didn't matter to me; she was still on my mind, and I became obsessed." I nod in response.

"Just know I don't fucking like you going alone... But I will stay here with Julia, like you asked, because I understand what you are saying. But I swear to God, Mikey! You fucking die... and I'll bring you back from the dead and kill you myself."

Mikey laughs at me, but then we fall into a comfortable silence.

Chapter 19

Mikey

It's five minutes until midnight, and I am sitting outside of this abandoned-looking warehouse that is on the edge of the river. There are no lights around, no movement at all. I am the only car that I can see.

Where the fuck are these assholes?

I kill the engine and sit there for a second. My hands are still on the wheel, white as bone from my death grip.

I should text Kai and tell him to lock the doors and windows. To set the fucking alarm and stay close to Julia.

Then I picture her right before I left the house, sprawled out on my bed, wearing my Vortex hoodie, curled into the blanket. She looked so peaceful and calm.

The peace she feels with us aches in my chest. She never felt safe a day in her life until now. And that just fuels the rage in my chest.

I step out of the car, and the cold hits me immediately. I can feel the winter coming on strong in Chicago. I am honestly surprised the snow hasn't come yet. I pull my jacket closer into me as my boots crunch over broken glass and gravel. I reach the rusted metal door and see two shadows flanking it. They are broad, armed, and looking unamused.

One of them pats me down, fucking rough. His hands close around my ankle holster.

"Nice try," he grunts, pocketing my gun.

"I expect that back," I say to him, and he ignores me, just opening the door for me.

I walk in and let the darkness engulf me. Inside, it smells like mold and rust. The only light is a bare bulb swinging from a chain. It keeps flickering and buzzing constantly; it's like it wants to die, but De Luca won't let it.

Then there he is. The man of the hour, standing beneath the poor, lonely light. He is perfectly still in his tailored suit and his hands behind his back. He looks like he just got out of a board meeting instead of luring me into an abandoned slaughterhouse.

He looks me up and down with that cold, calculated smile.

"Michael Monroe," He says, drawing out my name to save every syllable. "You grew up."

I force myself to keep my shoulders loose and my chin lifted. I refuse to show fear of him. "That's what happens when you eat food," I reply with my smart ass remarks.

"Always did have a sassy mouth on you." He tsks.

I look him straight in the eyes. Now it's time for business. "You asked. I showed."

He chuckles softly.

"Oh, you showed," he murmurs. "Ten years late, but I suppose we can overlook that... given the circumstances."

I don't like where this is going. My instincts haven't screamed this loud since the night Kai found that bastard on top of our mother and beat him to a pulp.

"What do you want from me?" I growl.

De Luca lifts his chin, and two more men step out of the shadows behind me. The hair on the back of my neck rises.

"I want my daughter."

My heart stops mid-beat.

He steps closer, "You took something from me, Michael. Years ago, you took a life that wasn't yours to take. And recently..." He tilts his head and looks at me, "You took my Julia."

"I didn't take her," I bite out. " She was living on her own. And your men were using her, for their own sick pleasure, and then beating the shit out of her."

He laughs, a soft, dangerous laugh. "My people do nothing without my permission."

"What the hell does that mean?"

"You think my men showed up at the bar by chance?"

A pause.

"You think they just took it upon themselves to hurt her and fucked her?"

Another pause.

"No, ragazzo. Everything that happened to Julia was ordered by me."

My stomach drops.

He steps closer to me, the dim light showing off the sharp lines of his face.

"She was getting... sentimental... rebellious and forgetting her place. She was spending time in the wrong districts, with the wrong friends, and making the wrong choices."

He leans in slightly, "Girls like her need correction, structure, and discipline."

I clench my fists so hard that my nails draw blood on my palm.

"And what's your solution?"

"Well, marriage, of course. She was promised years ago to a powerful family. A lucrative partnership. It was an arranged marriage she had been promised to since birth."

My vision goes red.

"You can't just..."

His hand snaps out faster than I can react. He has a fistful of my shirt and yanks me forward until our faces are mere inches apart.

"I can do anything I fucking want," he whispers. "She is mine."

The last words detonate inside me, and I swing.

But before I can make contact, someone grabs my arm mid-strike, twisting it behind me. Pain burst up my shoulder, and I am forced to my knees. A punch cracks across my jaw, then another, until the metallic taste of blood floods my mouth.

De Luca watches, bored, while his men beat me.

A boot slams into my ribs, and I feel something crack. I choke on a groan.

Another kick comes... then another.

My vision starts to blur.

"Enough," De Luca says, at last.

I'm panting, bracing on my palms as blood drips from my mouth onto the dusty concrete.

He crouches down in front of me, watching me like I am a bug he is getting ready to squish.

"You owe me a debt," he says softly. "For the man your brother killed and for the daughter you are hiding from me, I let you both walk free and play hockey, now it's time to cash in."

He grips my chin, forcing my head up to look at him. "So here is how you will repay me."

Every muscle in my body goes rigid.

"You will bring Julia to me. She belongs with her family. With her future husband. And if you don't..."

He taps my cheek lightly. "... I will collect her myself."

A colder threat that he didn't have to speak wraps itself around me.

"And Michael?" He rises slowly. "That beating?" He smiles down at me. "That was a mercy."

The men step back, and the door screeches open behind me.

"Midnight tomorrow," De Luca adds. "Bring her home."

As I stagger to my feet, my ribs screaming, blood dripping from my jaw, I realize three things:

1. De Luca never wanted a debt repaid.

2. He wanted leverage.

3. And he will burn the world down to drag Julia back into his cage.

But that can't happen if I burn him first.

Chapter 20

Mikey

I stumble out of the warehouse, one hand braced against the wall while the other is holding my ribs in place. It feels like shattered glass grinding under my skin. My jaw throbs in time with my heart-beat, and blood is dripping down my neck.

Behind me. The metal door slams shut, ringing in my head like a cell locking and a countdown starting...

De Luca's words are echoing in my head.

Midnight Tomorrow. Bring her home.

My stomach twists violently, and I gag, leaning over and spitting a mouthful of blood onto the gravel. My vision is swimming. I slap the hood on my jeep to stay upright.

I should get in. I need to drive and go home.

Instead, I stand there just shaking and trying not to collapse into a crumbling pile of shit.

My mind goes back to Julia.

FUCK

Just the thought of De Luca's hands on her....

NO.

I dig my fingers into my hair, pulling at the roots. I try to take a breath, but it feels like I'm inhaling broken glass.

I won't let that happen.

I fucking can't.

I force myself into the driver's seat, hissing at the movement, sending a shock of pain through my ribs. My hands are slick with dried blood as I grip the steering wheel. I must look like hell... Fuck, I feel like hell.

The drive home is a blur of headlights and a pounding headache. Every turn feels too slow, yet too fast. My chest tightens. I keep imagining Kai pacing the penthouse, checking the clock, and glancing at the door.

And Julia...

Hopefully still curled up in my bed, breathing slowly, still smelling like me from my hoodie.

A sick twist hits me again...

I'm about to go home covered in her dad's personal threat.

By the time I reach the building, my vision is tunneling. I barely make it through the parking garage without sideswiping a column. The elevator ride feels like hours; each floor ding is too loud.

When I step into the penthouse, the lights are dim.

I can see Kai sitting on the couch, waiting for me.

When the door clicks closed, he turns and freezes.

His face... fuck his face. It is full of shock, fear, and the kind of anger that makes grown men pray.

"Jesus... Mikey." He's across the room in two strides, hands hovering over me like he wants to grab me, but is afraid to.

"What the fuck happened?"

I swallow hard... or try to. My throat feels like it got shredded by a cheese grater.

"Don't..." I breathe out. "Not loud."

His eye flicks instantly towards the hallway, to my room, where Julia is sleeping.

He nods once in understanding.

He hooks his arm under mine and guides me towards the bathroom. The second the door shuts behind us, he turns and glares at me.

"Mikey." His voice is a low, deadly whisper. "What did they do to you?"

I don't answer immediately. I'm too busy bracing myself on the sink as the room spins. Blood from my eyebrow and lip drips onto the porcelain.

Kai's reflection behind me is pure fury.

"They want her," I manage to get my words out.

His jaw snaps shut. "Who?" I look up, meeting his eyes in the mirror.

"De Luca. He wants Julia back."

Kai goes still. Absolutely motionless.

"...Back?" The one word is so soft it's dangerous.

I nod, "...He wants her back. You know damn well what that means."

Kai's hands curl into fists. "That motherfucker..."

"There's more," I rasp out, and his eyes lock on mine.

"He arranged a marriage for her. Years ago. She was his bargaining chip. He found out she was planning on running, so he sent his guys to find her and 'discipline' her." My voice cracks. "He... ordered it."

Kai's face drains of color, and for a heartbeat, he looks like he might kill someone, or collapse. Fuck maybe both.

"No," he whispers. "He's not taking her." He shakes his head violently. "He's not fucking touching her. He's not getting anywhere near her."

"He said he'll come for her..." I say quietly. "If I don't bring her by midnight tomorrow... he'll come himself."

Kai slams his fist into the wall, cracking the tile. "Over my dead fucking body."

I push off the sink, groaning as pain spikes through my side.

"We need a plan," I grit out. "And we need to keep her out of this."

Kai steps forward again, this time gripping my shoulder, careful but firm.

"We will," he says. "But first, sit your ass down so I can clean you up. You look like you got hit by a fucking train."

I almost laugh, but my ribs protest, so the sound comes out strangled.

Kai lowers me onto the edge of the tub, then starts gathering supplies– alcohol wipes, butterfly bandages, gauze– by the time he comes back, his hands are shaking with rage he is trying to contain.

He kneels in front of me and starts to clean the blood off my face.

"You're not dying on me," he whispers. "Not tonight. Not tomorrow. Not fucking ever."

I close my eyes. Thinking about the fact that Julia is asleep just down the hall, curled in safety that she doesn't know is seconds from shattering.

And I don't know how the hell I'm going to tell her the truth, or if I even should.

Chapter 21

Julia

A sound pulls me out of my sleep.

It's a low hiss of pain behind the door.

For a second, I am disoriented. I don't know where I am. The room is dark, the sheets smell like Mikey, and the panic that usually sits in my chest is strangely quiet.

But then I hear the noise again. This time, followed by a muffled groan and a sharp inhale.

I sit up in bed, my heart pounding out of my chest.

That was the sound of pain.

I slide off the bed. As soon as my bare feet hit the hardwood, I am moving towards the door. Everything in my body is screaming at me to stay in bed, that with the life I grew up in, danger lurks in every shadow... but curiosity shoves me forward.

The voices get clearer as I inch down the hallway.

"... He wants her back. You damn well know what that means." I hear Mikey say through groans of pain.

Her... they are talking about her...

Kai's voice comes next. "That motherfucker."

My heart is racing. Are they talking about me? Or is there another her that 'he' wants?

"There's more," Mikey says again. His voice is so hoarse, I can tell he is seriously injured.

"He arranged a marriage for her. Years ago. She was his bargaining chip. He found out she was planning on running, so he sent his guys to find her and 'discipline' her." Mikey continues. "He... ordered it."

Fuck! He is talking about my father. I just know it.

"No," Kai whispers. "He's not taking her. He's not fucking touching her. He's not getting anywhere near her."

His confidence in protecting me is so sweet, but unrealistic with my dad. My dad will do anything to get me to do what he wants. Is he the one who hurt Mikey?

I swear to fucking God I will kill every single one of my dad's men, and my dad, if they hurt Mikey.

"He said he'll come for her..." Mikey says, then pauses for a second. "If I don't bring her by midnight tomorrow... he'll come himself."

Someone hits the wall, and then Kai growls like an animal. "Over my dead fucking body."

I walk over to the kitchen and start brewing myself a cup of coffee. My emotions are all over the place, and I am going to get every ounce of information out of these men.

I grab my cup of coffee and head back to the bathroom, waiting to hear if they say anything more. There are several curse words and a lot of hissing or grunts, but no conversation.

I finally decide what I am going to do, and I push the bathroom door open.

Both of them freeze.

Mikey is sitting on the edge of the tub, his shirt off and blood smeared across his ribs and jaw. Kai is kneeling on the tile beside him with a bottle of peroxide in his shaking hand.

Mikey is the first to look up at me, his eyes blown wide in shock, then you see a wave of fear cross over them, and then they finally settle with guilt.

"Julia," he whispers my name. His voice sounds like he smokes two packs of cigarettes in an hour.

I don't answer him, I just look at him, his face is black and blue, his nose is bleeding, he has a cut on his eyebrow and his lip, then I look further, and his shoulder is bruised. Then I get to his ribs, they are swollen and bruised also. He is so injured that he won't be able to play hockey.

I feel like I can't breathe. My dad did this. My fucking father!

"What happened?" My question comes out thin and cracked. "Who did this to you?"

Mikey tries to stand up–of course, he does– but the pain hits him too fast, and he winces, grabbing the edge of the tub.

Kai rises instantly, blocking me, like he is trying to be the human shield to soften whatever truth comes out of Mikey's mouth.

"Julia," he says carefully, " you shouldn't be up. Go back to bed."

"No." My voice shakes, but I don't back down from him. "I heard you. Both of you. Just... tell me the truth... please."

Mikey's jaw clenches as he sits back down on the edge of the tub. "Julia," he tires again, his voice raw and vulnerable. "Please..."

"Is it my father?" I choke out the last words. "Did he do this to you?"

They don't answer, and the silence slices through me.

I grip the door frame, keeping myself upright when my legs want to collapse in on themselves. "This is because of me," I whisper. "He hurt you because of me, didn't he?"

Mikey shakes his head violently, as tears threaten to fall. "No. No, Julia... he didn't hurt me because of you."

Kai touches my shoulder, and I look over my shoulder at him. "He wants you back." He doesn't hide the truth from me. He never has. "And he's willing to hurt anyone who stands in his way."

The room starts to spin, my throat starts to burn, and my eyes start prickling.

Because of course he is... Of course, this is happening again... I'm dragging destruction behind me everywhere I go. I can never just have a life that is mine.

Mikey reaches for me with a trembling hand. "Princess, please come here."

I walk to him on autopilot. When I get close enough, I can see more bruises forming and the blood drying his skin... But something shatters me when I see his split lip.

"Mikey..." I crouch down in front of him and touch his cheek gently. "Why would you let him do this to you?

His eyes soften, full of pain, and it makes my chest ache.

"I didn't let him," he tries to say, but his throat is raspy. "But I also didn't fight back. Because if I did... if I escalated it... It would have come straight back to you. But in all reality, when he told me he was going to take you regardless, I swung on him first; this was the backlash and warning from him."

A tear slips down my cheek. "You got hurt because you were protecting me."

He looks at me with so much love in his eyes. "I'd do it a thousand times."

I hear Kai take a sharp inhale. I can tell he hates hearing it out loud, but we all know it's true; these men wouldn't hesitate.

I wipe my face with the back of my hand and then get the courage to ask the question I know I will regret. "What does he want with me?"

Mikey hesitates to speak, but Kai doesn't.

"He arranged a marriage for you. Years ago."

My blood runs Ice-cold. Arranged marriage? I knew my father was cruel. But this is something I didn't think he would do.

Mikey whispers, "He said it's been planned since you were born, and he is ready to get it back on track."

Stars burst behind my eyes as my heart drops into my stomach.

Not again.

Not again.

Not again.

He wants to marry me off to a family he can still control me with; he always wants to have a leash on me, even with my new husband.

I stumble backwards, but Mikey grabs my wrist. He is being so gentle, like I'm made of glass.

"Julia," he says, voice breaking, "look at me."

I do, and it fucking destroys me.

There is so much pain and fear in his eyes, but I also see so much rage he is swallowing for my sake.

"We're not giving you to him," he says, "I don't care what he thinks he owns."

Kai steps up behind me, pressing his body against my back.

"Julia," he murmurs near my ear, "you're safe here."

I look between them. I look at the blood, the cracked tile, and all the bruises forming beneath Mikey's ribs.

Safe...I don't feel safe... But I do feel something else... Fear, terrified, protective, loved, wanted... I feel many things, but safe is not one of them.

I cup Mikey's face with both of my hands again and force him to look at me. "Don't you ever...," I whisper, "Take a beating for me again."

His eyes flutter shut. "Too late," he breathes.

Kai's hand gently slides down my spine, grounding me right where I stand.

"We're in this together now," he says. "All three of us."

And I believe him.

Chapter 22

Julia

The moment the words stop, I feel something else rising in me.

They think we're done talking… but we're not. Not even fucking close. I step forward, blocking the door to the bathroom and crossing my arms over my chest.

"Okay," I say tightly. "I have one more question."

Two sets of eyes look up at me. Kai immediately looks worried, and Mikey… Mikey looks defeated.

I don't give them time to brace for impact.

"Why. The. Fuck." I say each word sharply, "Were you dealing with my father in the first place?"

Mikey blinks several times like I just slapped him, and Kai freezes.

Good. I want them frozen and scared. I want them to feel even a fraction of what's twisting inside my chest.

"I… uh…" Mikey stumbles over his words.

"We used to work for him," Kai blurts out. Both mine and Mikey's eyes shoot to Kai. Mine are full of shock, and Mikey's look like betrayal and fury.

"Wanna explain?" I ask.

"No, not really," Kai answers honestly.

"Well, regardless, it involves me. My father and my men. You will tell me."

"Ohh, am I your man now?" Kai wiggles his eyebrow at me, and I slap his chest.

"Not the time! Tell me what the fuck is going on." I am as stern as I can be with these two men.

Mikey runs his hands through his long hair, pulling it back into a messy bun on the back of his head.

"When we were sixteen, we got involved with the wrong crowd. We were trying to help our mom with bills, hockey, and all of that. Well, one day, Kai walked in on a guy raping our mom; she was beaten up, and he was having his way with a damn near unconscious woman."

Mikey sighs and looks up at Kai to make sure he is doing okay. A sad look passes between them.

"Well, I got Kai off of him, but the dude was unrecognizable. We got my mom to the hospital, and when we came back, the dude was gone. I didn't recognize him, because we were so low on the totem pole, but apparently, he was one of the higher-ups in your dad's ranks..."

Mikey stops and looks at me. My mind is racing, and my stomach is turning. I feel like I am about to be sick. When I was planning on running away, they were working for my dad. We were in fucking high school, and they were working on the streets, for my dad... I nod at him to encourage him to keep going.

"One day, I was meeting up with the guy who was in charge of us, and he 'accidentally' told me that 'Kai was on De Luca's hit list, a life for a life, he said. Well, there was no way I was letting anyone kill my brother, so I went to talk to your dad. We came to an agreement that he would spare Kai's life, but I owe him a favor to be cashed in at his convenience."

He stops taking another breath. I can see his hands shaking. I honestly don't know what emotions I am feeling right now. It's a hurricane in my head. I have rage for not knowing they worked for my father, and I have sorrow for the boys who had to work in that kind of lifestyle to help their mom. I was shocked that Kai killed a man with his bare knuckles at the age of sixteen. But most of all, the confusion that my father would strike that kind of deal. I have never heard of him 'doing favors' or anything like that.

"Well, when we were in the locker room yesterday at practice... We had a visitor... one of your dad's men. Saying your dad wanted to meet me at midnight, they would send me the address. I got the address and went there. I knew I had to go, or Kai's life was on the line, and I would rather die than let my brother die. So I showed up at a warehouse. Your father told me to bring you to him by midnight tomorrow, and that if I didn't, he would come to collect you himself."

I nod, not expecting anything less from my dear old dad.

"But what made me lose it was that he said he could do whatever he wanted with you, because you were his. I swung on him, but before I could make contact, his men were on me, and then this." He gestures up and down his body.

"Okay..." I say slowly. My mind is trying to find the right plan.

"First. We need to come up with a plan." My voice cracks at the end.

A plan. I need a plan to outdo my father.

The room goes silent after the words leave my mouth.

Kai breaks the silence first. He steps forward, eyes snapping up like I just suggested we all jump off the balcony.

"Julia, No. Absolutely not. You are not going anywhere near that man."

Mikey immediately jumps in. "I'm not letting you walk into the lion's den. I already fucking told him—"

"NO!" The words rip out of my throat.

Both of them freeze and stare at me.

Good. Because they've been doing all the talking and all the deciding.

I'm done being handled.

"You two don't get to make this decision," I keep my voice steady. "He isn't after you. He isn't trying to take you. This is MY father. My life. My problem."

Mikey flinches at my words, and Kai's jaw ticks dangerously.

"Julia," Mikey says, "you don't understand. I saw how he talked about you. The shit he implied... your dad isn't trying to 'talk' to you. He wants to own you."

My stomach twists, but I keep my chin held high.

"Exactly." I snap. "Which is why I'm not letting him blindside me again."

Kai drags a hand down his face, like he is five seconds from losing his shit.

"We're not arguing about this. You're staying here." Kai's tone leaves no room for negotiation.

I step forward anyway, going toe to toe with him.

"You think you can lock me away in this penthouse and hide me like I am some glass doll? I'm not a fucking hostage! You don't get to control me."

Kai looks at me, eyes flashing with worry. "You don't get it, little dove—"

"Oh, I get it perfectly," I cut him off. "You think you can protect me from everything. Well, news flash! You can't! Especially from him! You don't know him like I do."

That silences them. Hard.

I take a breath, forcing the words out before the fear wins.

"When my father wants something... he gets it. He has resources. Money. Men. The kind of power that never stops. If he wants me back? He'll get me. He'll destroy anything and anyone in his way."

Mikey's throat bobs as he swallows, and Kai's brows pull tight.

"So we don't run. We outsmart him."

Mikey lets out a harsh laugh. "Outsmart the head of the fucking De Luca crime family? Julia—"

"Yes," I bite out. "Because he expects obedience, predictability, and fear. He expects YOU to follow his orders." I jam my finger into his chest, "and he expects ME to break," emphasizing my words.

"So we give him what he wants."

Both twins' heads snap up at the same time.

"I'm gonna need you to clarify that part for me," Kai says.

I grab Mikey's burner phone off the counter and lift it up to them. "I'm assuming this is connected to my father?"

Mikey nods, but doesn't say anything.

"We make him think the plan is working," I say. "That you're bringing me to him. That I'm terrified and compliant."

Mikey's eyes widen slowly.

"You want me to lie to him," Mikey murmurs.

"No," I correct. "I want you to bait him.

Kai crosses his arms over his chest. "Bait him with what? A fucking good vibes playlist?"

I grab the hem of Mikey's hoodie I'm still wearing, and yank it off.

"This," I say simply. "It smells like me. Looks like I was wearing it. You drop it at the meeting point. You let him think I was there, and that I ran. That you lost control. Something that forces him to react fast."

Kai stares at the hoodie like it's a grenade ready to explode.

"... Holy fuck," he whispers.

Mikey meets my eyes, something dark and dangerous brewing behind his expression.

"If I do that, he'll send every man he has to hunt you."

"Bingo," I say. "That's exactly what we want. He'll panic and spread himself thin, trying to scramble the resources. That will buy us time."

Kai steps forward. "And while he's chasing your shadow... where the hell are you?"

"With you," I answer simply. "Both of you. Somewhere he won't think to look."

Mikey frowns. "And where exactly would that be?"

"Wherever you two went," I say softly, "When you were sixteen and scared, trying to keep your mom alive. Wherever you hid when you were working for him."

Kai's entire body goes still. Mikey closes his eyes like he's being dragged backwards through time.

"You... You want us to take you to one of those places...?" He whispers.

"Yes."

Kai runs a hand through his hair.

"You know we have money, we can take you anywhere. That's not a safe house, Julia... It's barely a roof."

"I don't need comfort, I need to be invisible."

Mikey shakes his head; I can tell he is getting overwhelmed, and he probably needs sleep.

"Julia... if he figures out we tricked him—"

"He won't," I cut in, "not until it's too late. And when he comes for us again, we'll be ready."

Silence falls again around us. But this time it feels loaded.

Kai again breaks the silence. I swear the man doesn't know how not to talk. "... Fuck. She's right, Mikey."

Mikey's head snaps up toward him. "You're agreeing with this? Are you fucking insane?"

Kai shrugs. "She's done running. And she's not wrong... De Luca expects her to fold. If she doesn't, we get the upper hand."

Kai then turns to me. "And if this is the plan... then we're doing it together."

Mikey exhales slowly, looks between us, then nods once. "Fine," he mutters.

My chest tightens with pride and a little bit of fear. These men, who could choose anyone in the world, are standing by me. Through my bullshit. Against him.

"Okay, then we have until midnight.. After that, we make him regret ever trying to own me."

The twins exchange a look. Looking something like, *for her, we choose war.*

Chapter 23

Kai

Julia's words won't leave my head.

We outsmart him.

I thought we were out of this lifestyle. Even after my mistake, I didn't know Mikey took the fall for that; I felt that they just let it be when we went into hiding with Mom. I guess I was fucking dumb and naive.

I'm pacing the kitchen, my bare feet padding against the marble in a dangerous rhythm.

My mind is circling around every way this can go wrong. One wrong move and I can lose not only Mikey, but also Julia.

I glance over to the hallway towards Mikey's bedroom. I keep thinking about Julia... She's safe... for now.

And god help me, I will burn the fucking world before I let that change.

"You still awake?" I mutter to Mikey. I need to know his head is on straight before he goes out to the pits of hell... Alone.

"Yeah," he answers quietly. "You?"

I snort, "Do I look asleep?" I stop my pacing and raise my hands at him. I am literally walking in circles... absolutely not asleep.

Mikey sits up on the couch and rubs his hands down his face. I see a small wince as he stretches; his ribs have to be killing him.

“I don’t like this,” His voice is soft through the tension in the air.

I freeze mid-stride and turn towards him. “Neither do I.”

Does he understand how much anxiety I have running through my body? My other fucking half is literally walking into the slaughter-house alone, trying to protect me. I'm a twenty-six-year-old man! I can fucking defend myself.

"She shouldn't be anywhere near this," he continues. "I have spent ten years trying to keep you out of this mess, and now this..."

"She's already in it," I cut him off. "Because of who her father is, this has nothing to do with us. And as for me, you don't have to protect me. I can handle MY stuff."

I see him wince at my words. Then he blew out a long breath, calming his nerves. “He wants to marry her off. Like she’s fucking currency. Like she is expendable.”

My molars grind as I forcefully hold in all my rage. "That's how he's always treated people. What's new?"

"Yeah," Mikey breathes out. "But not her, we can’t let him do this to her."

The silence settles through the room again, then the burner phone buzzes on the coffee table.

My eyes snap to the phone as Mikey slowly reaches for it. I walk over to the couch and read the message over his shoulder.

De Luca: Tomorrow. Midnight. Don't test my patience.

I stare at the screen, the words burning through my soul. I can't let him do this alone. How the fuck do I convince him to let me go with? I understand, Julia needs someone here, but still...

"I'm texting him," he says.

My spine straightens. "Now?"

"Yeah. Before he starts wondering and questioning me."

His fingers start to fly over the keys, barely shaking.

ME: I'll bring her. I'm trying not to scare her. Don't push this.

I watch every word, wondering and hoping that it will be enough. He should believe it. He has to believe it. "He'll believe that. He always had a fetish for fear."

"Yeah, he has." Mikey sets the phone back down. Now that the trap is set, we have to wait and make sure it sticks so that we can get away with this very unpredictable plan.

I got to get Julia to the old unit; it's the safest spot.

Mikey dragged his hand down his face. "You scared about the spot?"

"There's only one place he never knew about," I say. "And it's still off-grid."

"The old unit?"

I nod. We hid there for weeks with our mom when things got bad.

"If this goes sideways—" I start to say.

"It won't," He interrupts sharply.

I raise a brow. "You don't know that."

"I know one thing," Mikey says. "He doesn't get her, or you."

I watch him, then nod once.

"Okay," I say. "Then we do it your way." I don't like doing it like this. There are so many things that could go wrong. And it's not like we will just lose a game or get kicked out of the playoffs. This shit could cost me my whole brother.

I let out a breath and glance down the hall again. Julia... She has no idea that Mikey and I are setting everything in motion.

But that's good, she doesn't need to know everything right now. She deserves one more night of peace before everything detonates, and she becomes the main target of her father's wrath.

I watch Mikey grab the hoodie off the chair, the one she wore earlier, and tuck it into his bag. Then walk towards the door.

"Hey," I said softly. I turn and look at him.

"If this ends with him coming for us hard..."

"You know it will," he says. "But this is the way we get him to show his hand."

“But regardless, just know I love you.” I let the words fall out. We don't say it enough to each other, but that man walking out that door is the other half of my soul, and there isn't a damn thing in this world I wouldn't do for him.

“I love you too,” Mikey whispers, and he is out the door.

As soon as the lock clicks into place, my soul shatters, and a tear slips down my face. That might have just been the last time I get to see my brother alive, and that's not something I thought I would ever experience.

Chapter 24

Mikey

I pull up to the warehouse and put the Jeep in park. This place looks worse the second time. I can see more of the structure rotting away, and all the rust on the metal.

I grab the burner phone and my bag, then step into the cold air. My boots crunch on gravel as I walk toward the entrance.

I am hoping with everything in my body that this works. I need this to work.

I push open the already cracked metal door and step in before I hear a slow clapping echo through the space.

"Michael," De Luca's voice carries through the warehouse. "Always punctual."

He stepped out from behind a stack of crates, looking immaculate as always. He has a dark coat on with polished shoes, and not a speck of dust on him, even though we are in a place full of it.

Two men flank him, and three more fan out behind me. I don't turn around, but I can feel their stares on the back of my skull.

"I told you I'd bring her," I say evenly.

His head tilts to the side. "I don't see her, but I do see you brought something."

I slide the bag off my shoulder and drop it at my feet, and slowly unzip it. I pull out Julia's hoodie--My hoodie that she was wearing--and her phone.

I place every piece down on the ground carefully.

De Luca's eyes sharpen at the items and then look back up at me.

"She ran," I say. "She panicked. I tried to stop her." I twisted the lie in just enough truth to make it believable.

He steps closer, looming over the items, studying them like they are an ancient artifact. He lifts the hoodie and presses it to his nose briefly.

"She always did hate being caged," he murmurs under his breath. His gaze snaps up to me. "Where?"

"I don't know," I say. "Not exactly. She talked about leaving the city. Said she couldn't breathe here anymore. Said she has been planning this for a while."

He smiles at me, then. You can tell he is not pleased.

"You failed to control her," He says, dangerously soft. "That was your only task."

"I'm aware."

His hand comes out of nowhere, slapping me across the face. Pain exploded through my cheek, and I staggered. Blood fills my mouth, but I swallow it. I refuse to show him any weakness.

De Luca exhales, disappointed. "You should have broken her. Fear keeps women obedient."

My vision goes red at his comment. I will never make Julia fear me.

I keep my voice steady. "You told me to bring her. I couldn't drag her here without tipping her off."

"I guess you did what you could," he says. "Which means you're still useful."

His men step up behind me and grab my arms before I can react, then force me to my knees, with a loud crack as my bones hit the concrete. A fist slams into my ribs, and this time I can't hide the grunt of pain.

"This," De Luca continues calmly, "is what happens when you disappoint me."

Another hit... then another. They don't rush the hits; they pause between each one, stretching out the punishment for their enjoyment.

I focus on my breathing and staying conscious. I focus on the clock that is ticking in Kai's head until I return, on Julia asleep, peacefully unaware of the fact that De Luca is still invested.

Which means our trap is holding.

When they finally stop, I'm breathing hard, and my hands are shaking on the concrete.

De Luca crouches in front of me and grabs my chin, forcing me to look at him.

"You will find her," he says. "And when you do, you will bring her directly to me. Willingly... or in pieces. Do you understand?"

I nod once.

Once he is satisfied, he releases me and stands to his full height.

"One way or another, my daughter will come home."

They leave me there, bleeding and bruised, but alive, which was the goal.

I stay on my knees until I hear the last car pull away, then stand. I smile through the pain because he now thinks she ran, and he thinks he's chasing.

I just hope it's enough.

Chapter 25

Kai

The second Mikey walks through the door, I can feel something's wrong.

He is moving like he always does after a hit, but it's not the injuries that set me on edge... It's his face.

There's no real relief there.

I'm on my feet before the door clicks shut. "You good?"

Mikey shrugs off his jacket and hangs it on the back of the chair. "Yeah," he says too quickly. That's strike number one.

I grab his wrists before he can move past me. "Sit." He doesn't argue. That's strike number two.

He drops onto the couch, staring at nothing as I walk to the closet to grab the med kit. I've patched him up enough times to know the routine: ice, compression, and silence.

But since there is stuff that needs to be discussed, his wish for silence is going to be ignored this round.

"You saw him," I say. He nods once.

"And?"

He hesitates with his answer. My stomach tightens. Strike three.

"He bought it," Mikey says finally. "The runaway angle. The bait."

I pause, gauze halfway up his ribs. "Then why do you look like you just handed him a loaded gun?"

Mikey exhales slowly. "Because he didn't explode."

His comment makes me stop everything and look at him in confusion.

"He didn't scream. Didn't threaten to burn the city down. Didn't send his men out immediately to search for her." Mikey's jaw tightens as he continues. "He was kinda amused."

I finish taping him up and sit back on my heels. "That's not his style."

"No," Mikey agrees. "When he loses control, he gets violent. When he thinks he's gaining it--" he cuts himself off.

"He gets patient," I finish.

He nods, and a chill crawls up my spine.

De Luca's patience is worse than De Luca's anger. Patience means planning. Planning means traps layered inside traps. This whole thing means he thinks he's already won something.

"He didn't push for a location?" I ask.

"No. He just told me to find her." Mikey's eyes flick to the hallway, staring at the door, where Julia is sleeping. "Which means he thinks she'll resurface. Or that I'll lead him to her."

"Or," I say slowly, "he already has another angle."

Mikey looks up at me then... studying me. "That's what scares me."

I scrub my hand over my face and start to pace. "He wants her married, controlled, and untouchable." I stop pacing for a second and glance back at my brother. "If he truly believed she ran, he'd be tearing the city apart."

"But he's not," Mikey says. "Which means he's waiting."

"But the question is for what?" I raise a brow.

Mikey doesn't answer, because we both know... He's waiting for her to make a move... for us to slip.. for our fear to do the dirty work for him.

I lean against the coffee table and stare down the hall. Thank god she's still asleep.

"He didn't bite because he didn't need to," I say quietly. "He thinks the leash is still on Julia."

Mikey's jaw hardens. "Then we cut the fucking leash."

I nod once, "And we do it before he decides to yank."

We fall into an uncomfortable silence because now the plan isn't about hiding Julia; it's about staying ahead of a man who's always ten steps ahead and just proved he's willing to wait to get what he wants.

Chapter 26

Julia

I wake up to tense-filled silence. The kind of silence that feels stretched too tight that it might snap if I breathe wrong.

The bedroom is dim, with the curtains barely open. I can see the city outside, muted and gray. Mikey's sheets are still warm beneath me, and his scent invades my senses.

I sit up slowly and listen. There are no voices, no laughter... Nothing. Something is wrong.

I swing my legs over the side of the bed and wince as my bare feet hit the cold floor. I'm wearing Mikey's shirt now since he had to take the hoodie. It hangs off my shoulder and is down to my knees. I clench it tighter around myself and step into the hallway.

The penthouse feels different in the daylight.

It's clean and open.

A whisper of voices comes from the kitchen, not arguing, but also not calm.

"She doesn't know," Mikey says. "And she can't. Not yet."

My breath catches. Are they really trying to hide shit from me again?

Kai sighs, and I can picture him rubbing the back of his neck to try to ease the tension. "She's not stupid. She will pick up that something's off the minute she wakes up."

Mikey doesn't deny it.

My pulse is loud in my ears now.

"I just... I don't like how quiet he was," Kai says. "He's waiting for her."

I take a step back before I can stop myself, and the floor creaks softly beneath my foot.

Both voices cut off, and two sets of hazel eyes snap toward me.

"Julia?" Mikey calls.

There it is... the softness and concern in his voice. Like he is trying to bubble wrap me and make sure nothing in the world is wrong.

I step into view and force my face to be neutral even though my insides are shaking.

"Morning," I say quietly, walking into the kitchen to the coffee maker.

I can feel Kai's eyes on me, studying me to search for any cracks in my armor.

Mikey stands, slowly... and I see it instantly, more bruises.

My breath stutters. "What happened to you?" I ask.

Mikey opens his mouth, then shuts it.

Kai cuts in. "Practice was rough."

I look between them, as the heat blooms behind my eyes, I can feel the anger stirring, "You're lying."

"Julia--" Mikey says, sounding completely defeated.

"No," I interrupt, hugging the shirt tighter to me. "Don't. I can feel the tension. I can tell there are secrets you're not telling. The way you're both acting like I might break if you just fucking tell me the truth. It's fucking bullshit."

Neither of them speaks, and that's answer enough.

My stomach twists painfully. "Is this about my father? Is that what I can't know yet?"

Mikey's shoulders sag, and Kai swears under his breath.

There it is...

I swallow hard, but my voice shakes despite every effort I try to keep it steady. "You don't get to protect me by shutting me out, not after everything that we talked about last night."

Mikey takes a step towards me, "We're trying to keep you safe."

"And what happens when I realize you've been bleeding for me behind my back? And then you try to keep it from me, when I am right in front of you, seeing the damage?" I say as I run my eyes over every bruise he has on his body.

The silence stretches heavy in the air...

I wait, but they don't answer... And that's what breaks me.

"You don't get to do that!" I scream. Everything in me shatters. "You don't get to decide what I can handle and what I can't, especially when this is my father. My life and my mess!"

Mikey closes his eyes like my words are physically hurting him, and deep down, I hope they do. I am tired of this shit. They act like I am some fragile little girl.

When he opens them again, I can see all the guilt he is holding onto.

"Kai," he says quietly. "Give us a minute."

Kai hesitates, flicking his eyes to me, then back to Mikey. Whatever silent conversation they have, he finally nods once.

"I'll be on the balcony," He mutters, already moving towards the sliding door. "Yell if you need me."

The glass door shuts behind him, sealing us in the kitchen with all the things unsaid.

I wait there as the quiet presses in before I step closer to Mikey. I grab his face and lift my head, forcing him to meet my eyes.

"Tell me," I say. "Now."

He exhales slowly, "He didn't push... not the way I expected."

My stomach drops. "Push how?"

"He didn't demand that his men go search for you. He didn't threaten you outright." He drops his gaze. "He acted like you were already coming back."

Cold spreads through my chest, the way it always does, when my father is being a conniving cunt.

"Like I belong to him," I whisper.

Mikey's hands curl into fists at his side. "Exactly like that."

I swallow, forcing air that feels like fire into my lungs. "And you?"

He won't meet my gaze, and my temper spikes.

"And you," I repeat, sharper this time. "What the fuck did he do to you?"

"Julia—"

I turn his head to make him look at me again, "I saw the bruises. Don't fucking insult me by pretending that I didn't."

For a moment, he sat there and looked at me. Like, really looked at me. Like he's deciding whether telling me will hurt me more than not telling me.

"He wanted to remind me," Mikey finally says slowly. "That he still has a reach on me, and that I better not disappoint him again."

My chest aches. This man just took a beating because of my plan. "And you let him?"

"The goal was only to survive."

I shake my head, letting the anger, hurt, and fear tangle together until I can't even decipher which one is which. "You went alone."

"Yes."

"You didn't tell me."

"No."

"You let me sleep in your bed while you walked straight into the pits of hell."

His eyes snap to mine. "I would do it again."

"That's not fucking romantic!" I scream. "That's terrifying!"

He reaches out his hand for me, but doesn't touch me. Like he is scared I might shatter.

"I know," he says. "But letting him think you're unguarded? Letting him believe you might be running? That's buying us time."

"I know, but you should have told me you were leaving."

"I wanted to give you one last night of sleeping soundly. One more morning where you woke up feeling safe."

I look up at him, tears running down my cheeks. "And now? What's the next step?"

"Now, we move... fast." His voice is rough and determined.

The balcony door slides open behind Kai, and we step back in. You can feel the tension in him as he walks up to me. "He still hasn't made a move," he says. "Which means he's biding his time and watching."

"Then let him," I say.

Both of them turn to me.

"I have spent my whole life being controlled by fear of him," I continue, but feel my voice getting steadier by the word. "It's time I fight back and get my freedom for good this time."

Chapter 27

Mikey

"Alright, well, we need to go to practice, but you are coming with us," I say to Julia.

She turns slowly, eyes narrowing like she is preparing to argue. With how many beatings I've taken recently, I don't think I have the patience for attitude right now.

"Why?" She crosses her arms over her chest, tipping her chin up in challenge.

"Because I don't trust your father," I answer flatly. "And because you're safer with us, at the arena with the team. Not here alone.

“Well, yes, that. But why the fuck are you going to practice with everything going on?” You can see the complete confusion in her eyes.

“Because we have to pretend nothing is out of the ordinary for us, princess. If we do, your father will catch on,” I reply.

She studies my face, searching for a weakness that she can slip through, but there isn't one.

I've already decided. If she pushes this, I will physically carry her out of here, and she knows it.

When realization flashes through her eyes, she crosses her arms. "Fine." She huffs. "Let me get dressed. How long do I have?"

She looks to Kai first, then back to me. "We have an hour," Kai says.

I step closer to her before she can protest. I reach out and lift her chin with two fingers, forcing her gaze to mine.

"You're not leaving my sight," I say quietly. "Not for a second."

"Is that an order?" she asks.

I lean in, close enough that only she can hear me.

"That's me keeping you alive."

For a moment, something vulnerable flashes across her face, then she nods.

"Okay," She murmurs. "I'll be quick."

She walks by me and runs her hand down my chest, grabbing my dick through my pants. When I look at her, she just smiles and walks to my bedroom.

"Oh, it's on." I turn and run towards her, grabbing her around her waist, kicking the door open, and throwing her on my bed.

"We are going to be late," She squeals and laughs at the same time.

"Well, you should have thought about that before starting shit." I pull my sweatpants off and stalk towards her.

I hear Kai walk into the room, but I don't turn to look at him, my attention fully on Julia.

"You will hurt yourself," I laugh at her.

"I think I will be fine. I have had worse hits." I crawl up on the bed to her.

"I think she is asking for a spanking," Kai says behind me, "Trying to tease and then back out? That's not how that works, little dove."

"Oh, really? Is that what happens? I get spankings?" Julia says, and my eyes sparkle with mischief.

She sits up and scooches off the bed, then runs out of the room. Kai is after her in a second, his naked ass being the last thing I see. By the time I can get myself out the door, Kai has her over his shoulder and smacking her ass.

"You're about to get fucked, little dove."

"That was kinda the idea," She sasses back, and Kai smacks her ass again.

When they get into my room, she is thrown on my bed again , and Kai stomps over to my bedside table, pulling out my rope and running it through his fingers.

He looks at me for permission, and I shrug.

He turns back around to her and gets up on the bed, straddles her, and grabs one of her wrists.

As soon as he goes to tie the rope around her wrist, she starts to wiggle, and I can't help but laugh. I sit there and watch my brother struggle with our woman being a brat.

"Hey, voyeur, you gonna come help me? Or am I the only one going to tame our brat?" Kai is still struggling with a squiggling Julia.

When I walk over, I grab Julia and pull her so she is sideways on the bed. I grab her arm that Kai is not holding and take the rope and tie her hand to my bedpost. When I get her secured, I check to make sure it's tight, but not going to hurt her.

Then I walk over to the hand Kai has been struggling with, and tie that one next. Once I am done, I step back and watch to see what Kai's next move will be. I want him to take control of this situation because I know he needs it. With everything else going on in our lives that is out of his power, the bedroom is something I can let him control.

"Listen here, little dove, I am going to use you like the good little whore I know you can be." She pulls at the restraints and growls when they don't budge.

"Were you two Boy Scouts, also?" I can't help but laugh at her.

"No, we were not Boy Scouts. Hockey took up the majority of our lives." I brush a hair behind her ear.

"So this is how this is going to work, my love," Kai bends down close to Julia's ear, "Since I am already straddling you, I am going to fuck that sassy ass mouth of yours. And Mikey here is going to fuck that pussy so hard you can barely stand, let alone run from us again. We are going to show you exactly what we do with brats."

Chapter 28

Kai

I get off of Julia, admire Mikey's handy work, and smile down at her. In this angle, her head is hanging off the bed, perfect for me to fuck her throat nice and deep, and Mikey can do what he needs to do.

I grab my painfully hard cock and start to stroke it, watching her eyes track my every move.

Mikey climbs up on the bed and positions himself at her entrance.

I walk closer to her mouth and tap the tip to her lip. "You ready for us, princess?" She nods eagerly, and we both slam into her at the same time.

My dick hits the back of her throat, and I see her eyes start to water, but she doesn't gag.

"Oh, fuck little dove, you feel so fucking good." I pull out and slam my dick back in. Mikey and I find a rhythm with her body, moving in harmony.

"That's it, Princess. Your pussy was made to take my dick. Just wait until your pussy takes both of our dicks, you will be seeing a whole new universe that revolves around only us."

His words must have made her excited, because she swallows around my dick, and she starts to move her head to try to keep up with my pace. My breathing picks up, and I start to see stars. I pull out of her mouth and shake my head.

"Ah, ah, ah. I said I was fucking your mouth. You don't get to take control, little dove. "

"What if I want control?" She winks at me.

"Then I will fight you on it, and you will just end up with a raw throat and a red ass." Her mouth goes into the perfect oh face, and I slam back in, fucking her mouth relentlessly.

Drool starts to run up her face and make a mess of her hair. It's the most beautiful sight I have ever seen.

"Kai, I don't have much longer." Mikey grunts. I look up at him, and I know he can see it in my face that I'm about ready to blow, also. As soon as I see Julia's body start to tense up, I know she is about to cum. Next, Mikey goes undone, and finally, I let myself cum down her throat.

I swear I have never cum so hard in my life.

When I finally come back to Earth, I pull out of Julia's mouth; she swallows what's left, then licks her lips clean.

"You know how sexy you look, licking my cum off of your mouth like it's the most addictive thing you have ever tasted?" She shakes her head.

"Extremely. If we weren't on a time crunch, I would fuck you six ways to Sunday."

"Well then, I guess after practice, you will have to," she winks, head still hanging off the bed.

I reach over and start to untie her hand, as Mikey walks over to untie the other. As soon as she is undone, she sits up, and you can see her eyes go out of focus as the blood rushes out of her head.

I go to the bathroom, wet a washcloth, bring it back to Julia, and wipe her up gently before tossing it into the dirty clothes basket.

"Alright, little dove. Go get dressed, we gotta get to practice." I smack her ass as she walks past me to pick out her only pair of jeans she has here.

We have been washing them for her, because we haven't had time to go to her apartment and get new clothes. I make a mental note to take her clothes shopping after all this bullshit is over. We will also need to figure out what we are doing room-wise, because I know for a fact, I will not be sleeping without her for the rest of my days, and I can almost guarantee that Mikey will feel the same way, so we will need to get a bigger bed, and make room in our closets for her also.

Julia walks out of the bathroom a few minutes later wearing another one of my Vortex hoodies, her black jeans, and heels. Her hair is tied up in a twisty thing at the top of her head, and she looks completely refreshed and not freshly fucked. Which is bullshit, I might add. Because Mikey and I put in hard work to make her look freshly fucked.

"How do you walk in those things?" I ask before even realizing the words came out of my mouth.

"With more skills than you have." She sasses.

"You got that right." I can't even argue that logic; I would break my fucking neck wearing those death contraptions.

We get to the area twenty minutes before practice starts, so at least we have one small victory on our hands. We rush in, Julia getting dragged behind us, when I damn near run into Luca.

He stares down at me like I have six heads. "What?" I bark, pushing past him as we head to the locker rooms.

"Fuck." Mikey curses. Julia and I both turn to look at him, "We can't bring her into the locker room, but we also can't leave her here alone."

I turn my head back to Luca.

"Aye! Can you chat with Julia while we gear up?"

"What the fuck do I look like your babysitter?"

"No, you look like a ride or die, who knows we would do the same for you." He looks at me like I got him by the balls, before he nods and we run in, making quick work to change into our gear.

Chapter 29

Julia

I look at the tall Italian dude standing next to me, who looks pissed off at the world.

"You good?" I ask, trying to make small talk. I remember seeing him at the game that I went to with Mel, but right now he looks meaner somehow.

"Yup." He doesn't add anything else, just glaring at the locker room.

"Sure doesn't look like it."

"What the fuck is this? Twenty questions?" He snaps.

"Sorry, just making sure you were okay. Guess I'll just go find a seat." I start to walk away, and a hand pulls me back.

"Kai and Mikey said you stay with me. That means you stay with me."

I rip my arm from his grip, "Thanks, but I don't need a babysitter."

"Apparently, you do, that's why they asked me to watch you." I cross my arms and glare at Luca.

"You don't know anything about me," I snap.

"Then enlighten me, darling. Tell me why you have my best friends' balls in a twist and why the fuck they are now acting like protective dobermans around you. One wrong move and anyone could end up with their balls taken off."

"Maybe it's none of your fucking business." As soon as the last word comes out of my mouth, Luca grabs my face with his hand, squeezing my cheeks together.

"Listen here. Those two men in there? They are basically my fucking brothers! We have known each other since the first day we started kindergarten, we got our first pair of skates together, and have always been on the same team together. I know every single detail of the bullshit they went through growing up. So don't you ever act like what's going on with them isn't my mother fucking business." As soon as he is done, he lets go of my face hard.

My eyes go big at his words, and then it hits me. This man is what kept Mikey, Kai, and their mom safe from my dad and his men when Kai killed that man.

"I—I." I just stop trying. My words are failing me, and I feel like the biggest asshole ever.

"You don't know anything."

"I don't want them anywhere near this shit." He looks at me, shocked at my admission.

"What shit? What the fuck did you get them in?" His accusations cut me deep.

"My father... he wants me back. And apparently Mikey owed him a deal, now he is supposed to deliver me, and I know he won't, but if he doesn't, my father will kill me, and... " My words fall off. I can't tell him everything. I need to tell Mikey and Kai first, not this random stranger. Don't get me wrong, I get it. Best friends and all of that.

"And what?" I just shake my head. As soon as he goes to demand more questions, the locker room bursts open, and out comes my men.

"Thanks, man, we owe you." Mikey slaps Luca on the shoulder with his glove-looking thing. Luca nods and walks away.

We follow from a distance, then come out through a small tunnel that leads to their bench.

"You will sit here, while we practice," Kai says, and I nod—no point in arguing with these boneheads.

I sit down on the bench and cross my arms, trying to keep my body heat inside of me, since apparently I now get to spend my morning in the freezer.

How do these men like this shit?

I watch the ice as Mikey scrapes the ice with his skates and shuffles from side to side. Then he turns and leans his head on the net post and kisses it. I heard Goalies are weird... I guess my goalie isn't an exception.

The rest of the team is passing the puck back and forth and practicing power skating, skating faster than I knew possible up and down the ice. I watch with complete fascination.

I have never been a hockey fan, but I am a fan of the Monroe twins, so I guess that's the same thing.

I turn and look at Mikey again, and now he is sitting on top of his net, swinging his legs like a little kid. I laugh and turn to see the guys shake their heads at him.

Yeahhhh, that's my weirdo.

"Monroe! Get the fuck off your net!" the coach yells, and I can see the crinkle in Mikey's eyes from a smile.

I love that they are smiling. On the ice, it seems like they are finally free from the bullshit... my bullshit.

Practice goes on, and I watch them do things on Ice that I can't even imagine doing standing on non-slippery ground, let alone with a fucking knife on my foot.

Kai slams guys into the boards, but not as hard as the time at the game, and then he will skate by me and wink.

"Stop flirting, Monroe, and get your ass over here."

Drill after drill, they shoot pucks at Mikey, and he stops them. He is Mr. Miyagi.

I am standing outside the locker room, surprisingly, this time with no babysitter.

Luca walks out and looks up and down the hall.

"Come here," he nods his head to the side, and I follow behind him.

"Wanna tell me what the fuck you are hiding from my twins?" His twins?

I cross my arms, ready to give him a fucking earful.

"Don't start, diva. I know that you are hiding something, so spill it. And just know... I will know you are lying and find out regardless. So you might want to tell me at your own free will." He turns and looks back to the locker room again.

"I can't tell you," I say quietly, not wanting anyone to hear me.

"Why not?"

"Because you will tell Mikey and Kai, and I refuse to let them be in more danger because of me." Luca nods at me and then grabs my arm, pulling me even further down the hall.

"Mikey and Kai are my brothers. If there is anything that could put them in danger, I need to know about it. Right now."

I exhale and finally decide that I am not getting out of this. "Fine, but you better not tell them."

He raises his eyebrow at me in question.

"I swear to fucking God, Luca, I will cut your dick off and feed it to the fish." A low chuckle comes from him.

"Spill it."

"I'm pregnant." The shock on his face is apparent.

"Um.. excuse me?"

"SEE!" I throw my hands in front of me, gesturing to him. "This is why I didn't want to say anything!"

"No. It's fine. I need to know. But I just have a lot of questions."

"Okay, what kind of questions? Like how and when?"

"I know fucking how. And as much as I love those twins, I don't want to know about their dicks. I see them enough in the locker rooms."

I laugh a little, and it's nice to finally have a genuine laugh for the first time in a while.

"Mikey and I had a one-night stand when we first met. I am assuming that is the when. I don't have regular cycles, so I honestly didn't know until recently, when I tried to eat teriyaki chicken and threw it up. At first, I thought I just got some undercooked chicken, but then after that, all the chicken I ate made me throw up."

"Okay. Gross." He holds up his hand to stop me.

"Fucking baby." I roll my eyes at him.

"No, that's a fucking baby." He points to my stomach. I reach up and cover my hand with his mouth. "Will you shut the fuck up. What part of 'I don't want the twins to know' did you not understand?"

"Fine. So explain to me why you don't want them to know?" I cross my arms and give him an 'are you fucking serious look.'

"You know how fucking unhinged those two will get if they know, and the last thing I need is for them to do something stupid like go on a suicide mission after my dad."

"So we keep them away from your dad." He says this like it's the easiest solution.

"Yeah... when Mikey apparently owes him a debt? And my dad wants me for the payment? If my dad finds out I am pregnant, there will be nothing, and I mean nothing, to stop him from getting to me." Luca nods in understanding.

"Julia." I hear my name being called. I turn and see Kai and Mikey smiling at me.

When they walk up, Luca turns to look at them, his arms crossed, and a scowl on his face.

"Y'all want to tell me what the fuck is going on?" He asks them like a disappointed dad.

"Not really," Kai says as he grabs my hand.

Luca shoots up his hand and stops Kai from walking past. Could Kai push the arm away? Sure. But he doesn't.

"Okay, I'll tell you. but not right here." Mikey says.

"Meet you at your house." Luca agrees, and we walk out of the arena.

Chapter 30

Mikey

We are back home, and Luca is pacing our living room.

"So what you are telling me is... that the whole time we have been friends, you were dealing with the fucking De Luca's and didn't fucking tell me?" Luca is pissed.

"Yeah. We didn't think it was going to be a big deal... then it was. We didn't want to drag your family into it." I say.

"Drag my family into it? I am your fucking family. My fucking family is your family. Why didn't you come to us for help? You got yourself into a fucking shit show and now how the fuck do you expect to get out of it?"

"I don't know Luca. I was panicking, there was a fucking dead dude on my mom's bedroom floor, and there was a freaking hit out for Kai!" I am screaming, throwing my hands in the air.

"Okay, let's calm down. I get it, this sucks, but I really can't take the yelling, my head is starting to kill me." Julia walks up in front of me. I wrap my arms around her and bring her lips to mine.

She is always my calm during the raging storm in me.

"You're right, princess. That's the past, and we need to figure out what we are going to do moving forward."

Luca looks between Julia and me, then to Kai.

"So your plan is to go to the old apartment unit? The one I am pretty sure shut down because of infestations?" Luca raises a brow, and I just shrug.

"No. You will go to one of my family's safe houses. If they cross any line there, they are now stepping into my family's territory, and that's going to start a war they don't want. It will give you guys enough time to figure out a plan." I nod.

A loud ass bang comes from the door, and Kai looks at me at the same time I look at him. Who the fuck is at our house?

"I swear to fucking God if you don't open this mother fucking door so I can see my fucking best friend, I will castrate both of you and deal with the backlash from Julia with a smile on my face," Mel screams through the door.

Julia pulls out of my arms, grabs Luca by the arm, and runs to the door. She looks through the peephole, then gestures for Luca to open the door.

I chuckle because I don't know if she is doing it for her safety or if she is doing it to set up Luca and Mel to face each other again. Anyone could have felt that tension at the bar.

Luca opens the door, and Mel lets out a loud ass groan.

"MOVE!" She pushes her way into our house and scans the room. When her eyes meet Julia's, she runs into her arms.

"Bitch, what the fuck! You haven't answered my calls, my texts, my anything." Mel grabs Julia's face and looks it over like she is checking to make sure we didn't damage her.

"I am fine. I had to ditch the phone." Mel raises a brow to Julia.

"Why?" Mel looks back at Kai and me, throwing blame at the wrong people.

"Because my dad." As soon as the words leave Julia's mouth, Mel freezes.

"What the fuck do you mean because of your dad?" Julia then proceeds to go through the whole story with Mel about what's going on.

"So what's the plan?" Mel asks, cracking her knuckles like she is ready to take on the world.

"We are about to get ready to go to Luca's family's safe house and then work out a plan from there."

"Cool, let's get going then." Mel stands up and grabs Julia's hand.

I sit there blinking at them like I am watching a reality TV show. This woman didn't even blink at anything Julia said about her dad; she was just ready to go.

"Who the fuck said you can go?" Luca growls from behind me.

"I did, fucker. My best friend is in danger, and that's where she is going, so that's where I will be. Fucking fight me." Mel sasses back.

Luca rolls his eyes and then heads towards the guest bedroom door. "I gotta talk to my dad and get everything figured out. You guys get packed."

Julia turns towards Kai and me, looking at us with serious eyes. "What about practice and games? You even said yourself that you have a contract to uphold."

"Don't worry, we will figure it all out. The goal is to have this done sooner rather than later."

We get to the safe house, and I'm starting to freak out. I feel like everything is about to hit the fan, and that scares the shit out of me.

"So what's the plan?" Kai asks me.

"I got to meet up with De Luca, eventually." I sigh. The real question is: when is eventually?

The burner phone buzzes on the table, and I look over it. I am not even sure how to breathe right now.

"Let me go this time," Kai says, reaching for the phone.

"No," I say sternly. "I will not let my brother take this." They will not think twice about shooting him if he shows up instead of me.

"I can't lose you. You are the smart twin." Kai mumbles out, his voice softer than I have ever heard it.

"You are fucking smart, Kai. I made this deal. I will handle everything that goes with it. You need to take care of Julia." I don't look at him, just stare at the phone that will determine my fate.

Same warehouse, midnight tonight. Don't be late.

"I don't know what he wants. So you need to stay here with Julia. Someone other than Mel needs to be with her."

"You need to bring someone with you."

"If I do, it will raise suspicions." Kai groans. I know he hates this just as much as I do. This whole situation is fucked. But I need to figure a way out of this that won't get us killed.

"Fine," he says, walking away.

"I don't want to go as much as you don't want me to go." He stops mid-step and then turns, heat blazing in his eyes.

"You know what's going on from your standpoint. You don't have a fucking clue what is going on from mine. I have to stay in this fucking house and hope my brother comes back to me. Hope that I will still have a fucking twin, and hope that Julia still has the love of her fucking life coming back to her, also. You don't know what this feels like." He screams at me, his hands moving with every word he says, as tears run down his face.

There are very few times I have seen Kai cry, but this time has hurt me the most. I nod, not knowing what else to do. "I'm sorry, you're right, I don't know what that is like. But I can say I will always do my best to come back. You know that. We are a duo, always have been, always fucking will be. There is no you without me..."

Before I can finish my sentence, Kai wraps me in a big hug, and for a split second, I am stunned. "I can't lose you; we already lost dad, and that damn near killed mom. I can't lose the only family that has been through life with me." His voice is hoarse from crying, and fuck, I wish I could take his pain away.

"I will try my best not to get killed." He pulls back from me and looks over at the kitchen, where Julia is dancing with headphones in, completely oblivious to our conversation.

"You need to tell her." He nods his head to her. I rub my hand down my face. I don't even know how to tell her that I have to go out tonight. But he is right. I need to keep her in the loop and not try to protect her. She is just as much involved as I am.

I walk up to Julia and wrap my hands around her waist, and rest my chin on her shoulder. She turns her head and smiles at me, taking out one of her headphones.

"What's up?" she asks, then notices mine and Kai's faces, which still have tears running down them.

"What did I miss?" The panic is now showing.

"I got a text from your dad. I have to meet him again tonight."

"Why?"

"I'm assuming for an update on you, but I am not sure. I haven't said anything about knowing your whereabouts."

"You are going alone." She raises a brow at me. It's not a question, but more of a challenge.

"What am I supposed to do? Walk in with you and hand you over on a silver platter?" I ask with a half-chuckle.

"I won't go." She says sternly.

I kiss the top of her head. "I know, Princess, that's why I need to go alone."

"No!" she yells. "Take someone with you. Anyone. Take Kai, or Luca." She is rambling now, trying to get me to agree to anything.

I shake my head. "I can't. If I take Kai, who will you have?" She goes to talk, and I hold up my hand. "And don't say Mel. Because, as scrappy as she is, your dad's men can squish her with one ass cheek." She lets out a sigh in defeat, and I continue. "And I can't take Luca because he is a part of the Moretti family."

As soon as I say his last name, everything clicks into place. As much as the De Luca's have a pull on this city, the Moretti's have more. They are the top of the top here in Chicago. So bringing Luca along will only cause more problems, and they will assume that I am trying to cause a war.

"I understand... But, you can't go alone."

"Baby, I will be fine. I was fine the other two times. I will go in, let him know I am still looking, maybe tell him I got a lead, and then come back." I try to keep my voice neutral because, honestly, nothing with

De Luca is that easy.

Julia busts out laughing, and I look at her, completely confused. "Nothing with my father is that easy."

"Fine. I'll take Kai with me, but Luca and Mel are staying here with you." She looks at me, studying me, then finally nods.

I look over my shoulder at Kai, who looks just as shocked as I feel.

"I told you that I was going to go with you, and you told me no, she says the same thing, and you say yes! What the fuck is that bullshit?" He throws his hands out in front of him.

"It's called life." I shrug and look at Julia.

"Please stay safe for me." I bend down and kiss her, then walk away, pulling out my phone and texting Luca.

Me: I'm taking Kai with me; I need you here to protect Julia.

Luca: On it.

We are in Kai's truck, pulling in front of the warehouse, which I have been to too many times for my comfort, within the last week.

"Fuck, this place gives me the creeps," Kai mumbles under his breath.

"Tell me about it." I get out of the truck and walk around the front, waiting for Kai.

We walk up to the front, the guys there frisk us, and then we head in. Ever since that one time they took my gun, I keep it in the vehicle. I'm not losing out on my money like that again.

De Luca's laugh echoes through the warehouse until we walk into the dimly lit room.

"Oh, well, isn't this a treat for me." He taunts.

"What the fuck do you want?" I say to De Luca, wanting to get this bullshit over.

"Why in such a hurry, Michael? Got somewhere to be?"

"Probably going to find your fucking daughter as you asked of me." I feel Kai stiffen next to me. Hopefully, he can keep his face neutral because De Luca can pick up that shit like a hound.

"Well, that's actually why I brought you here." De Luca rubs his chin, like he is thinking of a master plan.

"I'm tired of waiting," he finally says.

"Okay? And that's my problem, how?"

"Because you are done searching for Julia. I have come up with a better plan." He looks behind us, and I can feel some men moving closer.

"And what is this plan?" I try to keep calm, but every instinct is telling me to fight.

"You, and now your brother."

"What the fuck does that even mean?"

"Well, you see, Michael. Julia likes to keep her toys. And I saw how cozy you three were together. So if you can't bring my daughter to me, I will use you, well, now both of you, to get her."

As soon as his last word leaves his mouth, I feel a hand touch my shoulder, and I swing. I hit the guy in the jaw and then turned to look at Kai. He is hitting another guy. I turn and take another swing at the guy when something hard hits me in the temple, and everything fades to black.

Chapter 31

Julia

"Luca! They haven't fucking called." I am pacing back and forth in front of the couch at the safehouse. Mel is sitting next to me, scrolling through the channels, ignoring Luca's every move.

"They will when they are done. We have to be patient."

"Patient? It's five in the fucking morning, the meeting was at midnight, how much more patience do I need to have? Because I am losing my mind right now."

The panic is running through me, I don't know how to think, what to do.

"I'm just.... I'm just freaked out. What if he killed them?"

"Calm your pregnant ass down and watch TV with your best friend." As soon as the words leave his mouth, I glare at him, and Mel looks up at me, shocked.

"Um, excuse me?" she says, now glaring at Luca.

"What do you mean, pregnant ass?" I run my hand over my face and then flip off Luca.

"Thanks, jack ass." I turn to Mel.

"I'm pregnant. Surprise."

"Surprise! Fucking Surprise? That's what you have to say to me. And why the fuck was this dip shit the first one to know and not your best friend?"

Luca smiles at Mel, smugly.

"I wasn't going to tell anyone until the twins knew, but this one," I throw my thumb over my shoulder, pointing to Luca, "basically forced it out of me."

"And you didn't think to tell me?" Mel stands up and throws her hands up in the air.

I roll my eyes at her dramatics. "I didn't have my phone... So how did you expect me to tell you?"

"True..." She looks back at Luca, then back to me. "Do you know how far along?"

"Well, I am assuming from the first night when I went to the bar alone."

"Okay... Okay, I got it." She nods.

I turn around from Mel, about to tell Luca to find my men, but he isn't behind me. I walk around the tiny ass house and find him standing in the bedroom on the phone.

"Yeah, all the cameras around that area and more. I need to find them. Find the truck." I stand there and listen to his conversation.

"Yeah, yeah, right the fuck now. They have been gone for five hours. Yeah, I'll send you the address." He ends the call and turns, meeting my eyes.

"So you are worried, but want to play big and bad?" I cross my arms and glare at him.

"I am trying to keep things calm."

"Well, I am not calm." I snap at him and throw my hands in the air. I know I shouldn't be yelling at him; it's not his fault, but it's hard to hold back my temper.

"I noticed," he raises his brow at me.

"So, what's the plan?" I cross my arms again. If this fucker keeps up his smart assness, I'm gonna let my temper fly.

"I have a guy looking into the video footage to find out where the guys are, and figure out what kind of backup we will need. There is a lot of planning to do, but something isn't sitting right with me." I nod in agreement. Something isn't sitting right with me either.

"Okay, well, let me know what you want me to do."

"I want you to stay here; you are pregnant."

"And I want you to go fuck yourself. I am not staying here like a sitting duck. That's not how I work."

"I know it's not, but I had to try. You know the twins will be pissed if you come with me."

"Does it look like I care?" I know at this point, I'm being rude, but I don't care.

"When they get pissed at me, I will throw your ass under the bus." The fact that I know he would stick to that makes me laugh.

"Alright, deal."

Chapter 32

Kai

I wake up, and my head is pounding. I feel like I got hit by a damn semi truck. I go to rub the ache on my head, but my hands won't move. I try to look around, but my eyes are blurry. I blink several times before they clear up.

"What the fuck," I groan, pulling at my wrists. They are bound together. I try to twist my wrists to feel what it is... Handcuffs.

Mikey is tied to a chair right in front of me, still passed out, head lolling to the side.

Where the fuck are we? How did we get here?

That's when the memory of the warehouse rushes into my brain. We are bait... for Julia. I hope she doesn't fall for it. I hope that she can see through this bullshit and doesn't do anything rash.

Fuck Luca better have her.

When I finally get myself calmed down about Julia possibly coming after me, the hot, burning rage starts to settle in.

De Luca. This mother fucker took me and my fucking brother to lure our girl in. It's fucking bullshit. I pull at my wrist again, the handcuffs biting into my wrists, until I feel the drip of blood slide down my hand. I look at Mikey and see a chain wrapped around his waist, down his legs, and around the chair, securing him to it with no wiggle room. I look down at myself and see myself similarly bound.

Guess the mother fucker doesn't want me to kick the shit out of him. Out of all the things De Luca is, dumb is not one of them.

I start looking around the room to assess the bullshit we are in. It's a concrete room, and a metal table is next to us, with restraints on it. Then again, the far wall is lined with cabinets. There are chains, some with meat hooks, some without, hanging from the ceiling. There is a drain in the center of the room as well.

This is the kind of room that you see in horror movies where the serial killer will cut off a single piece of your body and watch to see how long you drain out. I want to hang fucking De Luca from these damn meat hooks and watch him drain.

I hear a groan from Mikey, and my attention shifts to him.

"Holy fuck." He groans, blinking his eyes several times to get them to focus.

"Yeah, kinda the same reaction I had," I mumble. He looks at me, and his eyes go big when he sees all the chains wrapped around me.

"I'm good. Don't pull your wrists; they are handcuffs, and they are tight." I try to move my arms to show him mine that are still dripping blood.

I watch Mikey as he takes in the room; the only difference is that his face is full of horror at everything he notices, whereas mine is still filled with rage.

"Do you remember anything?" he asks me.

"I remember everything up to you getting hit. Once you got hit and fell, I went to fuck up the guy who hit you with a fucking lead pipe, and I got hit also. Too bad it wasn't Mrs. Scarlet from Clue, at least she would have been hot." Mikey rolls his eyes at me, and I try to shrug.

"Okay, so we are in a fucking torture dungeon, with no clue about anything."

"Yup, basically."

"Dude, I'm so sorry, I should never have brought you with me. This should just be me here, not both of us."

"Mikey, shut the fuck up!" I yell at him, I can't handle this shit.

"I love you, dude, and I am glad I am here, and you aren't doing this alone. But stop with the pity party, and let's figure out a plan to get out of this shit hole."

Mikey nods, and then a loud ass squeak comes from the door behind me. That's fucking uncomfortable being back to the door. Mikey's face turns to rage.

"Well, isn't this just something?" De Luca's voice booms through the room.

I roll my eyes, and Mikey growls. "What the fuck do you want?"

"Well, Michael, you already know that answer. I want my daughter." He pulls up a chair that I didn't see sitting next to the wall, and straddles it, staring at the blank wall across from him.

"You see. When you told me that my daughter ran, I believed you at first. It's absolutely something Julia would do... but then I got thinking, and the way she looks at you two... She wouldn't have left you behind." He rubs his chin like he is thinking, then turns to look at me.

"And what an honor it is to have Mr. Malachi Monroe here, also. It is truly an honor to meet the man who, as a child, killed my second in command with his bare knuckles. Such a big task for a young man."

"I can show you how it was done if you want a replay," I growl.

"Oh, I am sure you could. But for right now, I would like to just talk."

"I got nothing to say to you," I say. "You can go fuck yourself with a fucking cactus dildo."

"Such a mouth on you. At least your brother knows when to shut up... sometimes."

"So sorry for your luck." I spit at him, and he smacks me across the face. Mikey growls out at him, and I smile.

"You hit like a bitch." I say, trying to keep his attention on me, all he does is stand up and walk out of the room, not giving us even a glance.

"Do you really have to antagonize him?" Mikey glares at me.

"What? It's true." I try to shrug as much as the chains will let me.

"Stop it," he snaps at me.

"If he is hitting me, he isn't hitting you."

"I don't care if he hits me." Mikey spits.

"But I do!" I look up at him. "I will always take the hit for you. You have had to keep me in line my whole life; the least I can do is take a slap or a punch for you."

"Kai..." Mikey starts.

"Stop. I will not back down from this fucker. He can do all he wants, as long as you and Julia stay safe." I will take anything for these two. They are my whole life, and nothing will change that.

"I'm the one who is supposed to be protecting you from him." His voice breaks.

"Well, plans change. So get over it. You..." I get cut off by the door slamming open again.

"I'm backkkkk." De Luca sings as he walks over to us.

"Oh great..." I mutter, then I feel someone slap me upside the head, like I'm a fucking child.

I turn my head, and I can see the guy who hit Mikey with the fucking lead pipe. Tall, probably pushing six foot five, and has to be sitting at three hundred and fifty pounds of pure fucking muscles. He has a shaved head with tattoos covering it, and a black goatee to match his black eyes.

"Couldn't handle your own fights?" De Luca laughs when that man turns and punches Mikey in the stomach. His fist hit the chain, driving it deep. Mikey lets out a low grunt and pukes all over himself and the concrete ground.

My eyes go big, and I shut the fuck up. No way in hell is my brother taking hits for me.

"Nothing else to say, Malachi?" De Luca taunts as he crosses his arms.

I just sit there, not even acknowledging his existence. Fuck him.

I feel the rage starting to run through my veins. This fucker will die, even if it's the last thing I do.

"So, boys, we are going to play a game." De Luca straddles the chair again and leans against the back.

"I will ask a question, and you will answer it. Simple as that."

I huff out a laugh. Nothing is ever that simple, especially with this dumb nut.

"Okay, first question. Where did you meet my daughter?"

Neither of us answers, and tall and broody punches both of us in the stomach.

"Okay... so we are doing this the hard way." He taps his finger on his lips like he is thinking.

"Where is Julia?"

Again, we both don't answer; this time, the punch comes to the face. I groan, and I can feel my nose break with the impact.

"I will get answers, or you will end up being dog food."

Chapter 33

Julia

We are headed towards some random house in the middle of nowhere. Luca's IT guy was able to hack into the cameras and see that my dad took both men, unconscious, into the back of a blacked-out SUV. He followed them to this house.

Luca has a plan, but of course, it involves me sitting behind him and hiding. I know it's for the baby's safety, but it still makes me feel useless.

"We have to be as quiet as possible, going in. We can't risk you." Luca says from the passenger seat of the SUV. I nod at him, not having any words to say to him.

He reaches back and hands me something black. "Put this on." I grab it and examine it. A bulletproof vest: I take off my sweatshirt, slide it over my head and arms, and tighten the velcro straps, since I'm significantly smaller than Luca. Then place my, Kai's, hoodie back on.

"You and Mel better have a vest also," I say, looking to Mel, then Luca again.

“We have some. Worry about you and my nephew inside you.” Mel says without looking at me, pulls back the slide on her Glock 43, lets it go with a sharp click, then holsters it to her leg, grabs a second one from the bag on the ground between us, and does the same again, but putting this one in a chest holster.

“How do you know it's a boy?” I reach down into the bag and pull out a Glock 43X, smaller, but it is only as a last resort for me. Mel went deep diving down the interwebs and saw that shooting can be done while pregnant, but she said she would prefer me to use a knife.

“I just have a gut feeling. I am the aunt after all,” She says. I nod and pull back the slide and let it snap forward, the click echoing through the SUV, and then put it in my leg holster. I reach back into the bag and find a stiletto knife and a switchblade. I grab both and put them next to me.

“Luca, what’s the ETA?” I am getting impatient.

“About five minutes.” I nod at him and start messing with my nails. I am trying everything in my power to calm down and not go in guns blazing at my father.

How fucking dare he take what is mine! If he wanted me, he could have come talk to me himself and not sent his goons to have Mikey do it.

The rage is settling deep in my gut, but when I place my hand there, I remember that I have more than just me to remember about. This little bean inside of me is more important than anything else.

"We are parking a couple of blocks away and going to walk the rest of the way. Make sure to put your silencers on; we will have to kill the guards first, and don't want to announce ourselves." Luca is commanding the car like he has done this a million times.

I pull out my gun from my holster and bend down to grab a silencer from the bag. Luca grabs my arm.

"Not you." I raise a brow at him, "the fuck you mean, not me?"

"Keep yours holstered unless necessary; it won't fit in your holster with it on. Let Mel and me do the shooting." I glare daggers at him, but I know he is right.

"Fine, but I am the one to kill my father." He looks at me for a long moment, then nods.

"You ready to be badass bitches?" Mel asks while bouncing in her seat.

"You do realize we are killing people?" I raise a brow.

"I hope so. I need to get some of this pent-up rage out and put it to good use." I shake my head and chuckle. Leave it to Mel to make me laugh as we are sitting here getting ready to walk into a shit storm.

"Okay, Harley Quinn, have fun with that." I roll my eyes.

The car comes to a stop, and we all get out. There is a second SUV parked behind us, and men in black suits flow out of it.

"They are my guys," Luca says, calming my nerves just a bit.

"We are going to go around back. Julia, stay with me. Guys, you know what to do." All the guys nod in unison.

Luca grabs my arm, and we start to walk down the sidewalk, Mel trailing a few steps behind. I look back at my best psycho, and she is smiling and bouncing like a kid getting ready to walk into a candy store.

"Hey, little psycho, get your ass up here." Mel bounces up next to me, her blonde ponytail swinging with her step. We are all dressed in black to make it less obvious, but with her blonde hair, we stick out like a sore thumb.

"Okay, so what's the plan?" Mel asks.

"We go in the front door and find my brothers," Luca says with so much determination it hurts. "We will kill any man in our way, restrain De Luca, and let Julia do what needs to be done." She nods and grabs my hand.

"We are going to get them back, babe," She whispers, and all I can do is nod, not feeling anywhere near as confident as they are.

Luca stops outside a run-down house. It looks like a one-story house with a basement. Vines are running up the side of the house, the concrete walkway leading to the door is cracked, and as soon as we turn, a man standing there falls to the ground. A bullet hole through the head, bleeding all over the ground.

My stomach turns, but I hold it down. No time to pussy out now. I can handle blood.

We walk through the front door, and Luca starts to feel around his pockets for something, when he pulls out a lock-picking kit. I reach out and turn the door handle, opening the door. I turn and raise a brow to him, and he rolls his eyes.

Luca takes the lead and walks into the house, his gun drawn as he looks around every corner. I laugh; he looks like the main character in a spy movie.

"Come on," he whispers and waves his hand, leading Mel and me further into the house. We pass a living room to our left, furnished with all pristine white couches and love seats. To our right is a formal dining room with a solid oak table. We are heading towards the kitchen, which has an old-school black-and-white square-tile floor that completely clashes with the rest of the house.

I guess this house doesn't have to make sense if he just uses it to kidnap people. We walk through the kitchen that screams 1950s. It's not even just the checkered floor; it has teal-blue cabinets, lime-green walls, and an old-school double stove.

I am looking around the kitchen like I am in a museum when I run into a solid wall of muscle. I look up and see that Luca has stopped, his hands are slightly shaking, and he is staring at the door to our right.

The only other door is one with a window, and you can see that it goes outside.

Mel walks up to the door first, opens it, then turns back to look at us.

Luca finally steps forward and takes the lead, walking down the stairs. The stairs are old and rickety, and make you claustrophobic with the concrete walls that surround them; you can barely see the bottom. We reach the bottom, and it's a hallway with several doors on each side.

What the fuck is my dad doing with some horror movie shit in the basement?

We hear a laugh that sends a chill down my spine, and makes my skin crawl... my dad.

Luca picks up his pace, and we make it to the end of the hall, in front of the last door to the left. His and Mel's guns are drawn, and I pull out my switchblade and flip it open, ready to take on whatever is happening behind this door.

I look up from the blade that I am flipping around, and I have two sets of eyes staring at me. I can see both of them checking me to make sure I will be ok. I give a slight nod, and then Luca slams the door open, Mel follows, and then I am the last to enter.

I look around the room, and I see Mikey and Kai facing each other, both of them are beaten up pretty badly. Then there is Reyes, standing tall and smiling at me. He is to the left of them, his knuckles are bloody and bruised. Then, to the right is my dad, straddling a chair, looking like he is watching his favorite show.

"See!" My dad stands up, hands raised like he just won something. "I told you she would come. But what a surprise to see a Moretti here and whoever this is." He gestures to Mel.

"Let them go," I say, trying to push my way in front of Luca.

"Now, dear daughter, you know I won't do that until you are fully in my care again. Now tell your dogs to back off." I finally push in front of Luca and stand in front of my father.

"I'll come back home, but the four of them are to be set free." I stand firm.

"NO!" I hear Mikey growl, and then a fist meets flesh.

Before I can process anything, Reyes falls to the ground. I turn around, and Mel is blowing off her gun, like in the movies.

I blink, and Luca is pulling me behind him just in time to miss my father reaching for me. Mikey and Kai are screaming and fighting against the chains, and Mel has her gun pointed at my dad.

His hands go up, and he steps back. I have never in my life seen my father surrender, let alone to a girl.

"Now, let's not be hasty." He says with an unamused chuckle.

Mel steps towards him, and he takes another step back.

"Give me the key, Dad." I stick out my hand.

"I don't have it on me," He laughs again. I swear I have never hated his laugh so much in my life.

"Luca, go with him to get the key, please." Luca nods his head, then steps out of the way for my dad to walk by.

As soon as they are out of the room, I run up to Mikey and Kai, hovering my hands over their broken and bruised faces. Tears are running down my face.

"Oh my god, I'm so sorry, this is all my fault."

"None of this is your fault, princess." Mikey's voice is strained.

"I won't lie, I deserve most of this for all the fucked up shit I have done in my life," Kai mutters.

I shake my head hard, "No, you don't deserve this. This is all my fault. If I had never left him and just done what he said, this wouldn't even be a thing, and you two would be safe, just playing hockey."

"Baby girl. We were wrapped up in this long before we met you. It just so happens your dad found something on me."

Before I can say anything, the door opens, and in comes my dad, followed by Luca.

I stick out my hand, and my dad drops the key into my hand. I pocket the key and nod to Luca. Without a second thought, he shoots my dad once in each of his legs, and my dad crumbles to the ground.

"So I am going to make this very clear to you, father dearest." I bend down in front of him, but far enough away that he can't grab me. "If there is anything at all that I learned from you, it is that you don't touch what is mine." I point over to Mikey and Kai. "Do they look untouched to you?"

My dad just sits there, not saying anything. I swing out my hand, holding the switch blade, and slice across his cheek. He hisses at the pain, and I smile. "There we go. Now you are bleeding also."

"The next thing I learned from you is that love is earned, not just given freely." I punch him in the face, feeling the bones of his nose crack under my knuckles. I want to shake out the pain in my hand, but I don't; I can't show weakness here.

"And the last thing I can tell you, one-hundred percent learned from you, is to make sure when you kill someone, make sure to give them a little something to regret when they pass." I smile down at him, my blade still in my hand, with a tint of red on his cheek.

"Aren't you going to ask me what it is you will regret?" I raise a brow, and he spits at me.

I stand and cross my arms, "Well, that's just rude. But I'll tell you anyway, because I am feeling generous. You will regret that you never got to see your grandchild. " He laughs his manic laugh at me. "You act like you are already pregnant with the baby." His words break off.

"That's because I am." I smile at him, grabbing him by the hair and running my blade over his neck, as hard and as deep as I can. He looks at me and smiles as the blood pours down his shirt and onto the concrete floor.

As soon as I hear him take his last breath and the light leaves him, I feel a sense of peace, like my life is finally mine again.

I drop his body and kick him away, turning to my men, who are both looking at me with wide eyes and complete shock on their faces.

Chapter 34

Mikey

I look over at Julia, my jaw damn near on the floor. The amount of emotions running through me is unheard of. Not only did she kill her dad like some bad ass in a movie, but she also dropped a fucking atomic bomb on me.

She is pregnant... Is it mine? Not that it matters, because genetically, Kai and I are the exact same. But when did she find out? Why is she here if she is pregnant? What the fuck is going on? How did they find us?

The questions don't stop, as Julia hands Luca the key. He walks over and undoes the chain attached to the floor. First Kai's, then mine. I get up, and my legs wobble, but then Julia is there, tucking herself against my side and grabbing Kai on her other side, holding us up.

"What the fuck was that?" Kai says. I turn and look at him, then see Julia smile.

"Surprise..." She tries to shrug under our weight.

"Surprise? That's all you got to say?" My voice cracks at the end.

"What do you want me to do? Fall to my knees and ask for forgiveness?" Luca laughs behind us. I turn and glare at him.

"You fucking let her come here while she is pregnant?"

"You try telling that little hellfire, no." He bites back. He isn't wrong, telling Julia no is impossible.

I turn back around to her and wrap her in a hug, bringing her head to my chest, and kiss the top of it. I feel Kai behind her, sandwiching her between us in our perfect little bubble.

She looks up at me and wraps her hand around my neck, kissing me gently, like I might break, then turns her head and pulls Kai down the same way.

"Alright, love birds, as much as I love seeing this family reunion, we've got to go." Luca crosses his arms, looking impatient as ever.

As soon as I pull away from Julia, I miss her touch already.

I grab her hand, and we follow Luca out of the house. When we exit the front door, I see several of his men standing there with a gas can and one of them holding a box of matches.

"Light it up, boys," Julia's voice sounds so confident; it fills me with pride.

The men start to douse the house, and as soon as we turn the corner, the whole thing is engulfed in flames.

"Well, that took really fast," I say. Julia looks up and smiles at me, "Good thing this house isn't near any others. This place looks like it used to be a cute neighborhood, and then it was abandoned. It makes sense why my dad chose it."

We get into the SUV and head back to our penthouse. Everyone is quiet, minus the low hum of some rock music.

"I'll get someone on the paperwork about your dad's death." Luca turns and looks at Julia. She nods, but doesn't look him in the eyes.

"Hey," I lift her chin with two fingers to get her to face me. "What's going on in that pretty head of yours?"

She smiles at me softly, then sighs.

"I am just... trying to figure out life right now. It doesn't feel real. I am the last remaining De Luca." A tear slips down her face.

"Yeah. You are, and in my opinion, the best looking one also." Kai says from her other side, making her slightly chuckle.

"I just don't know what to do with my life now. My whole world has been following my dad's rules, then it was about not pissing him off, then avoiding him. What do I do now?" Another tear slips down her face.

"Whatever you want, baby," I grab her face again. "You have the whole world at your fingertips, and we will gladly stand here and watch you conquer whatever you want to."

Julia starts to sob, and my chest tightens. "What's wrong, baby? What did I say wrong? I take it back."

She shakes her head, confusing me even more.

"I—I am just so glad to have you two... well three... I think." She reaches down and places her hand on her stomach, rubbing slow circles. Kai reaches over and places his hand on top of half of her, and I reach out and put my hand on the other half of her hand.

"My family," Julia whispers, and my heart jumps out of my chest. I look up at Kai, and I can hear him say in my head, *Our family.*

Chapter 35

Kai

We walk through the front door of the penthouse, and the first thing I do is scoop Julia into a bridal carry.

"Put me down. You are hurt," Julia squeals as I walk her towards the bedroom.

"I'm never that hurt, little dove." I wink at her and keep walking. The pain is barely even there now. I know I will feel it after a night of sleep, but with all this adrenaline still running through my system, I will put it to good use.

"Never that hurt to do what?" She looks at me, confused.

"To fuck the shit out of the mother of my child." I give her a gentle kiss, then push the door to Mikey's room open with my foot.

"I swear to god if you hurt yourself more because of this, I will be pissed." She crosses her arms and gives me an adorable attempt at a scowl.

"I promise you right now, little dove, there will be many times in our lives that I piss you off," she smacks my chest, and I laugh. I mean... I'm not lying. I will piss her off more times than not, but she will have to deal with it because I refuse to live a day without her.

I lay her on the bed and start to strip off my clothes, ripping my shirt off my head, and then unbuttoning my pants. I can see in my peripheral vision that Mikey is also stripping. We are about to take this woman to a whole different universe.

Julia reaches down for the button on her pants, and I quickly smack her hand. She looks at me, confused, "Don't open my present," she laughs, and then lies back, waiting for me.

I am completely naked within the next two seconds. I climb up and straddle Julia, pulling her upper body up so I can take my hoodie off of her, then I pull off her shirt and unclasp her bra.

When she is finally naked at the top, I give her a deep, passionate kiss and work my way down her neck.

I feel the dip of Mikey joining us on the bed, and move off of Julia so he can take off her pants.

I kiss down Julia's neck, making my way to her beautiful breasts. I lick around her nipple until they are stiff points, and then I suck them into my mouth. I grab and massage the other tit, not letting either one go without some love, because man, I fucking love her breasts. I can't wait until they are full of milk. I swirl my tongue, and Julia moans, arching her back.

"Lift up, princess," Mikey says, and she obliges. I let go and move to the other tit, nipping, sucking, and playing with her nipple. She is a wiggling mess under me.

"Kai..." She moans out.

"What's up, little dove?" I lift my eyes to look at her.

"I need more," she whines.

"Don't you worry your little mind with that one. Let Mikey and me take care of you," I look over to Mikey, who is face-first in our girl's pussy, eating it like a man on death row. When he looks up, I raise a brow at him, and he sits up licking her juices off his lips.

I lie back on the bed and glance at Julia with a smile. “Hop on.” She rolls her eyes, swings a leg over me, and eases herself down on my cock without breaking eye contact.

"Alright, princess. My turn. I'll go slow." She nods to Mikey. I reach up and smile at her, grabbing her face in my hands and kissing the fuck out of her.

I feel Mikey's lubed-up dick slide along mine as he slowly pushes into her very wet pussy.

When he gets the head in, I can feel Julia tense against me. "Relax, baby. We will make you feel good."

She nods, taking a deep breath and lying on my chest.

Mikey inches in more, slowly, until he is fully seated. She stretches so perfectly around us; it is euphoric.

"Oh fuck. I am so full." Julia moans.

"Are you ready for us to move?" Mikey whispers in her ear. She nods, and we slowly start to move.

This is not the first time Mikey and I have taken a girl like this, but it is the first time that feelings were involved. And when I say that it makes everything feel so much better, I am not exaggerating.

"I need you guys to move faster." Julia pants out, and Mikey and I start to pick up our pace. Her pussy is so wet that it's dripping down my balls.

"You feel so good, little dove. You are the perfect missing puzzle piece to our life." I say, in between my panting breaths.

"Fuck, fuck, fuck." She screams out as her pussy clamps down on us. She is so close, and so am I.

"Come for us, princess," Mikey says, and she explodes around us. I follow suit, cuming harder than I ever have. As soon as I feel myself breathe my first normal breath, Mikey slides in one more time and finishes also.

Julia falls onto my chest and Mikey onto her back, still very much inside of her.

"That was..." Julia starts.

"Incredible?" I interrupt her.

"I was going to say intense, but incredible works also." We all laugh at her.

Mikey rolls off of Julia and flops onto the bed, then Julia rolls off of me. I get up, get a wet wash rag out of the bathroom, and come back. I wipe the inside of Julia's thighs and clean her pussy.

Before I am even finished cleaning her up, she is passed out.

I smile and put the rag in the dirty clothes basket, and then get back in to snuggle my woman.

She rolls over and pushes her ass against my stomach, and I start getting hard again.

Fuckkk, what is this woman doing to me?

I try to think about anything other than her ass on me, and slowly my dick starts to go down.

I sit there and let my mind wander about everything that has happened recently.

"De Luca is dead," I hear Mikey mumble.

"Yeah," is the only reply I can come up with.

"Julia is pregnant." Mikey mumbles, again.

"Yeah," I reply again. I think my brother might be in shock. I keep letting my mind wander, then Mikey shoots up in bed.

"We need to marry her." I blink at him like he has lost his damn mind.

"What?" Making sure all of my shock is apparent in the one word.

"We need to marry her." He repeats.

"Yeah, I heard you, dumb nuts. But you know just as well as I do that she can't legally marry us both."

"No, she can't, but she can legally marry you." I sit up, resting my head against the headboard as I stare at my brother.

"What do you mean by 'legally marry me'? You know she won't go for that." He must have gotten hit by De Luca's dude harder than I thought.

"Well, if the timeline is correct, she got pregnant by me the night we fucked at the bar. So most likely the baby is mine, well ours, but you know what I mean. So it only makes sense that your name be on the marriage certificate. We will both be her husband, but according to the legal system, it's you and her." He has thought this all through.

"And you are okay with that?"

"Yeah, it's just a piece of paper, but this way, no one can try to claim her based on some stupid mafia-arranged marriage bullshit because she is already married."

"And you think that will stop the mafia?" I question.

"Can I? No, but we have people who can. Luca wouldn't let anything happen, and did you see how pissed he was when he saw us chained up by De Luca?" He isn't wrong. Luca will kill anyone for us.

"Alright, let's say we go along with your plan. Where are we going to go?" I am skeptical, but trying to hear him out.

"Vegas." He smiles at me.

Chapter 36

Julia

"Where are we going?" Mikey and Kai just smile at me, like they have something up their sleeves. They are sitting across from me on this private jet. I turn and look at Mel sitting next to me, and she won't even make eye contact with me. I look over to Luca, who is ignoring us, swirling his whiskey.

"I'm just saying. All of you guys are now on my list!" I say, pointing to each one of them.

"Long as I am at the top." Kai winks at me, and Mel glares at him.

"If anyone is at the top, it's me!" She snaps, and I bust up laughing.

"What the fuck did I do to deserve to be on the list?" Luca finally looks up.

"Because none of you will tell me what's going on, and you." I point to Mel, "First hand, knowing I fucking hate surprises."

She smiles at me and shrugs. "Well, you kept the pregnancy from me, so call this Karma." I roll my eyes, pull out my Kindle, and start reading.

"Ohhh, what literature do we have this time?" Mel leans over and looks at my Kindle.

"Go fuck yourself." I snap and pull my Kindle away from her eye-view. She reaches out to grab it from me, and we start wrestling on a plane, laughing so hard that my stomach cramps.

"Hey, don't squish our baby." I hear Mikey yell, but Mel and I continue to wrestle around.

"Ohhhh, hockey smut. I dig it." She grins at me, and I roll my eyes and continue to read.

"Why do you need to read hockey smut when you are living it in real life?" Kai wags his eyebrow.

"Because sometimes I like to live through someone else's reality instead of my own." I flip the page and continue reading.

"Ladies and Gentlemen, we've reached our destination. We will begin our descent and be on the ground in approximately fifteen minutes. Please ensure your seatbelts are fastened." The pilot says, and I try to look out the window over Mel's head, but she is purposely blocking me.

Kai leans forward and grabs my hand. "I promise, baby, you will know soon what's going on, but this surprise is important to Mikey and me, so please just be patient with us." I lean in and give him my best smile.

"I am not a patient person."

"Oh, trust me, we can tell." I scrunch my eyebrows at him and glare.

"But you will be patient whether you like it or not." Kai then smiles.

"I don't like you two teaming up against me. This is fucking bull-shit." I huff.

"Okay, sassy pants. We are here, so surprise is over." Mikey says as soon as we feel the wheels touch the ground.

We exit the plane, and an SUV is waiting for us. Two men in suits are loading up our luggage.

When I turn around, Mikey, Kai, and Mel are staring at me, like I am supposed to be caught on by now.

"I am too tired to deal with your bullshit," I grumble, and get into the SUV.

"You know, usually people would ask where we are at," Mel says as she scootches in next to me, followed by Kai. Mikey gets in the passenger seat, and Luca starts up the SUV.

"Well, I know you ass-holes won't tell me, so why bother?" I lay my head on the window, and the airport starts to disappear, and the Vegas strip starts to light up.

"Why are we in Vegas?" I ask. Kai and Mikey smile at me, again hiding something from me.

"We have something to show you," Mikey says. I raise a brow, not buying what he is saying.

We keep driving, and I subconsciously start rubbing my stomach. I can see a little bump now, but it looks like I have just eaten one too many tacos.

I have never been to Vegas, so I have no clue which hotel we are pulling up to. I just know it's fucking huge. Mikey gets out of the car and opens my door for me, as everyone else follows us. Luca tosses the keys to the valet.

Kai walks up to the front desk and talks with a beautiful blonde lady, who is obviously flirting with him. I feel the jealousy show its face. Then Kai says something, and she turns to look at me, her face dropping. I give a little wave to piss her off more and grab onto Mikey, making my claim known.

When Kai gets a couple of key cards, he walks back to us, cheesing hard at me. "That was fun."

"What was?" I scowl.

"Turning down a woman because I am no longer single." I blink at him, confused.

"What do you mean?" I say.

"Well, knowing that you are ours, you are carrying our child, I would say that I am off the market, wouldn't you?" He questions me. I smile at him and reach up to grab his cheek and kiss him hard on the lips.

"I love you." The words slip out before I can stop them.

"I love you too." Kai bends down and kisses me again.

I then turn to Mikey, who looks like he just won the lottery. "I love you, Mikey."

He picks me up and spins me around. "I love you too, princess." When he sets me down, he grabs my face and kisses me.

"Okay, love birds, give me my key. I'll meet you in an hour." Luca goes to grab the key, and Kai pulls it back...

"Soooo there was a problem." He gives a sheepish smile to Luca.

"What kind of problem?" Luca's voice drops to a dangerous tone.

"They double-booked your room, sooooo surprise you will be sharing one with Mel."

"What!" Mel and Luca scream at the same time.

"Yeah. So here are your keys.... Have fun." Kai turns and grabs my hand and damn near drags me down the hall away from Luca and Mel.

"What did you do, Kai?" I look at him, trying to catch my breath, when we stop running.

"I was tired of the tension between the two, so I got them to share a room. Just call me matchmaker Kai."

"Dude, are you sure this won't be a double homicide?" Mikey butts in.

"Nah, they will be okay. Let's go to our room and freshen up." I grab both of their hands, and they walk me to the elevator at the end of the hall, and Kai scans the key card, taking us up to the top floor.

When the car dings, the elevator opens directly into a huge living room.

"You know, I never understood why you needed a living room in a hotel." I laugh. My dad used to always get these suites, and he would tell me it was so he could watch TV.

"Well, in this instance, we have more rooms to play in." Kai winks at me. I walk to the bedroom, see the suitcase Mel packed for me, and open it.

This damn thing is full of different lingerie outfits and toys... I roll my eyes, because of course, she would pack toys... like I don't have two men to keep me plenty busy.

Something blue catches my eye. I move the lingerie out of the way and pull out a beautiful sapphire blue strapless dress, with a deep cut in the front to show off my cleavage. It is fitted at the top and then flares out at the bottom, with a cut up the leg. It is stunning.

I hang up the dress in the closet and dig through to find some beautiful silver heels. As much as my best friend drives me nuts, she knows how to dress a girl.

I walk back into the living room, and both of the guys are sitting on the couch watching the hockey game. They are on a bye week, thank god. They haven't missed any practices or games during the time my dad decided to stir up bullshit.

"How do I need to dress?" I ask, and both of their heads snap to me.

"If I have it my way, I would say in your birthday suit. But I don't think Luca and Mel want to see us fuck the shit out of you." I roll my eyes at Kai and turn to Mikey.

"Whatever you want to wear." I look at both of them, dressed in suits, but neither has a tie; the top buttons are undone, and they look sexy as sin.

I turn around and walk back into the bedroom, pulling the blue dress from the hanger and laying it on the bed. If they are going to dress up, so am I. I dig around through the suitcase and find a curling iron and makeup. Perfect.

I go to the bathroom, apply my makeup, and tame my curls with the curling iron. When I look up at the mirror, I finally feel human again. I walk back into the room and pull on the dress and heels, then check myself in the mirror one last time.

As soon as I walk into the living room, Kai's mouth drops wide open, his blonde hair falling in his face, and Mikey instantly stands up. He starts to walk towards me, and I finally get to admire his whole look. His blonde hair is pulled back into a neat bun; he is wearing a navy blue suit, a white button-up shirt, and dress shoes.

Kai stands up next, his hair is down, hanging around his face, and he is wearing a black suit, a black button-up shirt, and dress shoes. I smile at them and do a spin to show off the dress.

"How do I look?" Both men are damn near drooling, and I laugh, physically pushing up their jaws and laughing.

"Come on, Luca and Mel will be waiting for us, if they didn't kill each other first," I say, then walk out of the hotel room.

Chapter 37

Mikey

When we reach the lobby, Mel looks ready to murder Kai.

"How dare you!" She spits out at him. Julia walks up to her and grabs her by the arm.

"Come on, fire cracker, I'm thirsty and want a Shirley Temple."

I continue to watch Julia walk away, her ass looking amazing in that dress.

"What's the plan?" Luca asks me.

"Well, now we go up to the rooftop, propose, then go get married." He looks at me like I have four heads.

"How do you know she will say yes?" He questions.

"Really? I wouldn't have dragged everyone out here if I didn't think that she would say yes." Luca huffs out his frustration as Kai chuckles beside me.

"So who's going to marry you?" Luca keeps throwing questions at me.

"Elvis or you." His eyes shoot up at us.

"We will go grab the marriage certificate, then everything will happen."

"When do you plan to get this damn licence?" Luca grumbles, already annoyed with this whole situation. He'll get over it.

"Right now, go keep the girls busy, and I'll be back," Kai says as he rushes out the door to the valet.

"You don't have to officiate if you don't want to, just thought you would prefer to do it instead of Elvis." He shrugs, then starts to walk towards the bar.

We pull up chairs, and he orders two whiskeys on the rocks.

"So I have to ask." I look up at him, waiting for him to continue, "Are you sure about all of this?"

I give him a small smile. "Yeah. I am. She is it for me." He nods. The bartender sets our drinks down, and we both grab our glasses and take a healthy gulp.

"I'm happy for you." He looks up at me, longing in his eyes.

"What's up, man?" He is like a brother to me. I know when something is wrong, just like I do with Kai.

"I am just happy to see you both in love. I will get there eventually," he chuckles and takes another drink.

"What about Mel?" I ask. I know something is there, but neither will admit it.

"What about her? She is annoying, bossy, and a brat ninety percent of the time?" He groans.

"So, it sounds to me like your soul mate." I laugh, take another sip.

"Yeah... No." He shakes his head.

We continue to have regular conversations, and then Kai comes running in. Huffing and puffing like he just ran a marathon.

"You sure you play hockey? You sound a little out of shape," Luca teases.

"How about you shut the fuck up!" Kai returns.

We all turn and look at the ladies sitting in a booth. Julia is talking about something; her hands are flying everywhere as she tells her story. When she feels our eyes on her, she turns and looks, smiling and waving us over.

"So, are these the big plans?" She asks me directly.

"No, love, it's not. Whenever you are ready, we can go." She looks to Mel, who nods at me and then grabs my hand.

We walk to the elevator, and I push the rooftop button, and then smile down at Julia. She smiles at me and then reaches for Kai's hand.

She notices the Manila envelope and raises a brow.

"You guys are hiding something, and I am not okay with it." She looks directly at Kai with daggers in her eyes, and all he did back was smile mischievously.

"Not much longer, little dove, just try to be patient with us." She rolls her eyes and looks forward, ignoring everyone in the elevator.

We exit the elevator and walk through the hallway. Right before we get to the door, I let go of Julia's hand and wrap my hands over her eyes. Mel opens the door, and Luca rushes forward, turning on all the fairy lights and the big sign in the back that says "Marry Us?"

"If I fall because I can't see, it's your fault," Julia grumbles.

"You know I will never let you fall," I whisper to her.

Mel walks over to me and takes my hand, and Kai lets go of Julia's hand. We walk over to the big sign and drop to our knees.

We hold a ring together, a 0.70 Carat G-VS2 Ideal cut radiant diamond garland sapphire and diamond engagement ring in platinum. We got the big diamond in the middle and a sapphire and a ruby on each side of the diamond to represent both Kai and me.

I give Mel a nod, and she drops her hands. Julia blinks a couple of times, and then her eyes focus on us. I smile up at her, and the emotions on her face make my stomach twist.

"We may have just met a few months ago, but you are the only person I can think about day and night. We have already been through hell and back, and now you are expanding our family. Let's make this official. Will you marry us?" My voice breaks near the end, and she smiles at me.

"You love me. You tolerate my brother. Let's stop pretending this ends any other way." Kai says, and I glare at him, then shake my head.

Julia now has tears down her face, looking between Kai and me.

"Say yes, little dove," Kai says, and Julia starts to nod her head.

"Y—Yes. Of course, yes." She runs up to us and wraps us both in a hug.

Kai and I pull back, and both slide the ring onto her finger.

"Perfect." I lift her chin and kiss her.

"Now the rule is, you can never take that off," Kai says, and Julia chuckles, wrapping us in a hug again and not letting go.

"This was such a great surprise," Julia says through the tears.

"So you don't hate them anymore?" I question.

"Oh, no. I still hate them." She laughs, pulling back from us.

"Well... we have one more," Kai says, and she looks up at him, scrunching her brows.

Luca clears his voice and straightens his tie.

"Will you marry us, now?" I ask.

She blinks at me, completely shocked. "Right now?"

"Yeah... Luca can ordain it; unfortunately, you can't legally marry both of us, but we can do the ceremony with both of us, and I will be the only one on the certificate with you." Kai explains, and my stomach turns. I hate the fact that Kai is the only one who gets to marry her legally. I know that it was my idea, but fuck, this hurts worse than I thought it would.

"Wait." She holds up her hand to stop everyone. "I'm not marrying just one of you."

Her words send a sharp zap through my body, and I feel alive again. Just those words solidify everything in me. I grab her face in my hands and get her to look at me.

"Baby, you are only marrying him on paper. We have tried to find any backdoor way for you to legally marry both of us, but it's not a thing, unfortunately. But to the world, you are both of ours. There is no one in this world who will be able to take you from us. I will yell it from every rooftop and mountain if I have to. I will crawl on my knees to you in front of a crowd. I don't care, because regardless of anything, I will show the world you are mine, just as much as you are his."

She nods, then leans down to kiss me. "Well, stand up then. We need to get hitched." She smiles at us. Kai and I stand up instantly and grab her hands.

Luca stands in the middle of the words, holding his phone. Julia stands to his right with Mel next to her, and Kai stands to Luca's left with me next to him. He clears his throat like this is a business meeting and not a rooftop wedding in Vegas.

"We are gathered here," Luca says dryly, "because none of you listen to reason." I chuckle, Julia snorts, and Kai nudges me and smiles.

Luca continues, unfazed. "Julia agreed to marry two men who are allergic to communication. Kai agreed to feel feelings publicly... briefly. Mikey agreed to stop flirting for the duration of the ceremony."

I blink at Luca, confused, and raise my hand. "Um. No one said that."

Luca doesn't look at me, but replies, "You're doing great. Keep quiet."

The wind starts to kick up, lifting Julia's dress. Kai steps closer to her without thinking, placing a hand on her back. She looks up and smiles at him, and I follow suit, going to her other side.

"Marriage," Luca says, "is not about perfection. It's about choosing the same people over and over again, especially when they're unbearable." His eyes flick up to Kai, then go to me.

Kai snorts. Luca gestures to me. "You first. Vows."

I don't hesitate. I take both of Julia's hands and turn her to face me. The warmth of her touch steadies my racing heart.

"Julia," I start, trying to keep my voice easy, "I promise to love you loudly when you need it and quietly when you don't. I promise to choose you every day, even when you pretend you don't need to be chosen. I promise to protect what's ours-- and to never let you forget you're wanted." I smile at her, then continue. "Also, I promise to keep things interesting." Then I wink at her.

Julia's laugh breaks through the wind on the rooftop, tears threatening to spill down her cheeks.

Luca nods. "Kai."

Kai looks like he might bolt, but instead, he steps in. Julia turns her whole body to him, smiling at him. Kai doesn't take her hands at first, just looking at her like he's memorizing this moment.

"I don't do speeches," he says. "You know that."

She nods, and a tear slips down her cheek. He reaches up to wipe it with the pad of his thumb and then licks it off.

"I promise to be the place you land. To choose you when things get ugly, to love you even when I don't know how to say it right." There is a beat of silence. "And I promise not to leave you. Ever. You are stuck with me."

Julia swallows hard. Luca hands her a piece of paper with generic vows on it, but she doesn't look down.

"I was supposed to be temporary, a one-night stand. I wasn't supposed to fall in love, and I did. Twice."

I can't help the grin that spreads on my face, and she squeezes my hand.

"I choose you," she says. "Both of you. The chaos, the protection, the way you see me, even when I try to hide. I promise to fight for us. To stay honest. To stay." Then she turns and looks at Kai. "You are stuck with me." Then she looks at me. "And I will keep you on your toes always."

Luca exhales. "Rings."

Julia turns and looks at me with panic in her eyes. "I don't have rings for you."

I pull out another ring box and hand it to her. When she opens it, she sees two silver bands, one with a ruby and one with a sapphire.

"When?" She looks at me.

"We ordered them all online, and then Kai went and picked them up with the Marriage certificate."

She nods and slides the sapphire ring on my finger and the Ruby ring on Kai's, then wipes away her tears. Damn, she looks beautiful even when she is crying.

Luca lifts his chin. "By the extremely questionable authority vested in me—"

"Luca," I warn.

"—I pronounce you married." He steps back. "You may do whatever it is you've been doing this whole time."

I lean down and kiss Julia first. She is all warmth and laughter. Kai follows right after; his kiss is slower and deeper. You can tell that he is sealing this forever. He always told me he would never get married, but he just did, and I have never seen my brother so happy.

Julia grabs our hands and pulls us to the edge of the rooftop, and we look out at the skyline. Vegas is screaming, the lights are flashing...

And on this rooftop, we chose Julia, and she chose us... Forever.

Chapter 38

Julia

After the guys and Mel drink a few drinks at the bar, and I probably had about twenty Shirley Temples, I am ready go back to the room. I have been dying to strip these men naked and get my mouth on them.

I see Kai look at Mikey, and they both nod and stand.

"Alright, everyone, I think it's time we take our wife up to our room, so I can eat my dinner," Kai says, as he reaches under my legs and swings me into a bridal carry.

My cheeks are blushing red, but I still manage to lean back and see around Kai's arm, waving bye to Luca and Mel. "Goodnight." Mel gives me a small wave in return, and Luca raises his whiskey in a toast.

We make it up the elevator and to the room in no time. Mikey gets the door, and Kai walks me in. He sets me on the ground, and I feel his arms rub along my shoulders and down my back. He reaches the zipper on my dress and slowly slides it down. His knuckles lightly graze my back, sending chills down my spine. Then I feel his lips kissing down my spine.

Mikey walks up in front of me, grabbing the back of my head and smashing his mouth to mine. I moan into his mouth and open up for him. As we are kissing, he pulls a tie out of nowhere and wraps it around my eyes.

My other senses are in complete overdrive. I can hear them shuffling, the sound of Kai's lips pressing to my skin, and the rustling of a shirt, which I am assuming is Mikey's. I reach out and try to touch Mikey, but I can't feel him, and when I reach around to touch Kai, he is also gone. As soon as he lets go of me, my dress falls to the ground, and I am left in a white lacy thong.

"Seriously? I am blindfolded, and at your mercy; the least you can let me do is touch you." I groan.

"Don't worry, princess, you will be feeling us very soon," Mikey whispers in my ear, and then he bites down on my earlobe.

I stand there, not sure what they have planned, but trying my hardest to be patient. The want for them is burning through my body so much that I feel like I am about to explode.

Next thing I feel is hands wrapped under my ass, and someone lifting me into their arms. I feel around on their body and instantly know it's Mikey. Each of these men feels different and unique. To everyone else, they are identical twins who no one can tell apart, except that Mikey usually wears his hair up and Kai doesn't.

Mikey sets me on the bed, and I feel a dip on each side of me, of the guys getting on with me.

"Alright, little dove, you won't be able to see, and we won't allow a lot of touching. We want to see if you truly know us apart." Kai says, then a pair of lips are on mine.

"Mikey," I reply

Then I feel hands on me rubbing up my stomach and squeezing my breasts. It's harder, with a pinch on my nipples.

"Kai," I answer confidently.

"Alright, princess, we are going to kick it up a notch. Are you ready?" I nod.

"Words, little dove, use your words."

"Yes, I am ready," I whisper. My nerves are on fire right now, and I don't know what to anticipate.

Next thing I feel is fingers sliding up my thigh, the touch is so light, that I want to say it's Mikey, but as soon as they get to my center, the fingers are thrust into my hard. I arch my back and moan at the intrusion.

"Kai," I moan.

I get a kiss from Kai, "Damn, she is good."

Next, I feel a dick being pressed to my mouth, and I reach for it, wrapping my hands around the shaft, and instantly I know that it's Mikey. Kai is a little bit thicker than Mikey is.

I suck his dick further into my mouth and start to move up and down his shaft. He moans out, and I know I am completely right. Mikey is in my mouth right now.

He pulls out, and my mouth makes a pop sound. "Mikey," I say, smiling at them, even though I can't see their faces in return.

Several long agonizing seconds go by, and I start to feel around the bed, not knowing what is going on. When I finally feel the tip of a dick at my entrance. I wait, even though I want to scream at them to fuck me already.

In one slow thrust, Kai is inside me. I know that for sure. It feel so good and I moan out his name.

"How the fuck do you know it's me?" Kai asks.

"You and Mikey hit different spots in me." I shrug like it's nothing.

I feel someone lying next to me, and then I am being lifted and straddled over one of them. I feel the dick at my entrance, and I lower myself, moaning out Mikey's name as he fills me. Once I am fully seated, I lean forward, making it clear that I need both of them right now.

The tie is taken off my face, and I blink to clear my vision. I see Mikey under me, just like I thought, and Kai is behind me, rubbing lube on his very hard cock.

"Well, you're going to stand there and stare at me, or fuck me?" I look over my shoulder at Kai.

As soon as I turn my head back around to look at Mikey, I feel Kai's dick breach my ass. He rubs circles on my cheeks as he keeps inching forward, achingly slow. Why the fuck are they being so slow?

I push my ass back and make him enter me more. I am ready to be full.

"Impatient are we?" Mikey cock a brow at me.

"Very," I reply, leaning down and kissing him.

As soon as both men have me full, I start moving, pulling out of both of them, and then slamming back in at the same time. Kai gets the hint and starts to move on his own, as Mikey stares at me, like I am the rarest gem he has ever seen.

As soon as he snaps out of his gaze, he matches Kai's pace.

I can feel them hitting just the right spots together, and it is making stars dance in my vision.

"Harder," I say through ragged breaths.

They pick up the pace, and soon I am soaring off the edge. Completely spent.

I fall on Mikey's chest as he and Kai use me.

I can feel them getting close; their thrusts get faster and more sporadic. A few thrusts later, and they are both filling me to the top with their cum. Kai pulls out of me and lies on the bed.

"I love you guys, more than anything else in this world. " I say, when I roll off of Mikey onto the bed.

"I love you too." They reply in unison, and then sleep takes over.

Chapter 39

Julia

We pull up to the penthouse, still in post-wedding bliss.

We don't make it three steps into the house before I hear the click of a safety being released.

Kai's body goes rigid behind me, and Mikey's hand slides from my waist to my back. Guiding me behind him without a word.

I recognize the man in front of us. He was at my father's house a lot. Silas Romano. He is the head of the Romano crime family here. They did a lot of business together, not that I was supposed to know that. I was a sneaky child who liked to eavesdrop on conversations that were not mine to hear.

He's looking at me, staring at my feet, and working his way up until he stops at my left hand that now has my wedding ring on it. His eyes jump to mine, and they are now filled with fury.

"Wait," Romano says, and I can feel a person behind us. It's one of his men; he has a gun in his hands, but it's not raised. He is tall, in a black suit, and looks like a damn brick wall.

Kai's voice breaks me from my stare. "You brought weapons into my house."

That's what he asks? Forget the fact that they are here uninvited.

"Insurance," Romano shrugs.

Mikey laughs softly, "That's adorable."

A gunshot cracks through the room, but I can tell it's not from Romano's man behind me; this one comes from the balcony.

Glass explodes outward as one of Luca's men drops in like gravity itself, already on the move. Romano's guard goes down hard, his gun skidding across the marble floor, before I can process what just happened.

Chaos detonates through the house, and Kai shoves me back, holding onto my waist firmly.

"Bedroom. Now." He growls, but I don't move.

Romano spins, reaching for his own weapon, but Mikey is faster.

He crosses the room in three long strides, grabs Romano by the collar, and slams him into the table hard enough to crack the wood. I look to the side, and Luca's guy is still there, gun drawn, waiting for the signal from Mikey or Kai.

“You don’t threaten my wife,” Mikey growls. “You don’t get to breathe around my unborn child like that.”

Romano wheezes through Mikey, choking the shit out of him, but still manages a smile. “Your problem,” He coughs, “is that my son is still expecting what was promised to him years ago.”

Kai steps in and draws his gun. I blink at him. When the fuck did he get a gun? I didn’t feel it on him.

"Listen to me," Kai says. "That deal died the moment her father signed it without her consent. It died again when De Luca took his last breath, and you decided to walk in here like you owned the damn place? And it will stay dead."

Romano's eyes flick past Kai and lock on me. I step forward and feel the twins tense through the air.

"Julia..." Mikey starts.

"I need him to hear me," I say.

No one stops me, but Kai finds my hand. I bend down to get closer to Romano's face. Mikey has loosened his grip on his throat so he can breathe... for now.

"You want payment?" I ask, tilting my head to the side, studying him. "Take it from me. I'm ending this. Now."

Romano laughs. "You think you have the authority?"

"I don't think. I know I do," I stop and look at Mikey, then at Kai. "Because if you touch me, if you touch my family, there will be nothing left of your legacy." I take a second to watch him process my words, "Do you understand me?"

Romano doesn't answer, just keeps looking at me.

Kai presses the gun into his skull to make his point clear. "This is the last warning."

Romano looks between the twins, then around the room slightly. He stops at his man, dead and bleeding on the floor, then to Luca's guy, who has his gun down to his side now, but you can tell he is still ready for anything.

Romano nods slowly.

"This isn't finished," he says hoarsely.

The front door opens with a loud bang, causing me to stand instantly, and in struts Luca. "Yes," he says, "it is."

He pulls out a gun and pulls the trigger. The shot tears through Romano's shoulder, not killing him. As Mikey releases, Romano screams, clutching his wound.

Luca leans down next to Romano, "Listen here. You are leaving alive as a warning. Julia, Michael, and Malachi Monroe are a part of the Moretti family. You do anything to them, you will be declaring war on my family. Do you hear me?"

Romano nods and is then dragged out, bleeding and broken, by more of Luca's guys.

When it's finally over, my knees give out, and Mikey catches me. Kai kneels in front of me, running his hands over my face while his eyes frantically check for any injuries.

"Hey," he says, grabbing my cheeks in both of his hands. "You're okay. You're both okay."

I nod and press my forehead to his. "I didn't know it would come back," I whisper to him.

"What would come back?" He pulls back from me, looking at me, confused.

My heart is racing, and I look around the room to make sure they actually got rid of Romano. "The past," I whisper, scared that if I say it too loud, something else will pop its ugly ass face out.

Mikey kisses my hair. "The past always tries."

Kai's hand settles over my stomach, "But it doesn't get to touch what's ours."

Chapter 40

Julia

2 weeks later

We walk into the OBGYN office, Kai and Mikey squeeze my hands just a little tighter. I look down, then smile up at them.

"You guys okay?" I ask.

"Yeah..." They both say at the same time, hesitantly.

I shake my head and laugh. "Who would have thought NHL stars are scared of a doctor's office?"

"I'm not scared." Kai huffs out, like he is big and bad.

We walk up to the front desk, and the receptionist smiles up at us.

"Welcome in, can I get your name please?"

"Yeah, it's Julia De Luca," Kai growls, and Mikey scoffs at me using my maiden name. The paperwork hasn't fully processed my name change yet. The receptionist looks at the guys with concern in her eyes and then hands me a clipboard.

"Please fill this out and give it to the nurse when she calls you back." I grab the clipboard and almost drop it from its weight. Damn, did they need my left kidney also?

"Thank you," I say politely, even though my stomach is twisting from the nerves.

We move to the row of chairs along the wall. Kai sits first, legs spread, and his shoulders squared like he is guarding a door and not waiting for an appointment. Mikey sits on my other side, close enough that our thighs press together.

I balance the clipboard on my knee and start filling out the paperwork.

Name.

Date of birth.

Emergency contact.

I pause as my pen hovers over that question.

My brain starts screaming at all the what-ifs— what if something happens to me? What if I hemorrhage? What if they regret this?

Kai notices immediately. "Put me down," he says without hesitation.

Mikey snorts. "Like hell, I'm older."

"By four minutes," Kai shoots back.

"Still older."

I chuckle a little bit and write both their names down, squeezing them into the space.

A nurse calls another name. A door opens and closes. Somewhere down the hall, I hear a baby cry... the sounds slice straight through me.

My chest tightens, and I freeze. Everything is becoming too real. That sound is going to be mine. I am responsible for an entire human being.

Mikey shifts even closer, keeping his voice low. "You okay, Princess?"

I nod, but can feel the burning in my throat. "Yeah. It's just... a lot."

Kai leans forward, resting his elbows on his knees, and looks at me like the rest of the room doesn't exist. "Hey. Whatever happens in there, good news, bad news, scary news, we're not going anywhere."

The word *we* hit harder than I expected.

Are they just as scared? Are they having these same internal thoughts?

A nurse appears in the doorway, clipboard in her hands. "Julia De Luca?"

I stand, and both of them stand with me.

The nurse's eyebrows lift slightly like she is not going to let both of them in, then nods, "You can both come back."

Relief crashes through me so hard I almost fall.

We follow her down the hallway, and the walls are lined with newborn photos and smiling families.

Kai's hand shifts from mine to the small of my back, keeping me steady. Mikey stays close, his presence calming me. These two really don't know how much just standing next to me calms me and makes me feel safe.

As we reach the exam room, the nurse chuckles and smiles gently. "First ultrasound today?"

My heart stutters. "Yes," I answer.

I lay back on the bed and lift my shirt.

The room lights dim, and the tech pulls the curtain halfway closed before sitting in front of the ultrasound machine. She grabs a bottle of gel and shakes it before squirting some on my stomach. The cold hits me, and I flinch.

Mikey notices instantly. "Sorry," he murmurs, like this is somehow his fault. His hand tightens around mine, and Kai is hovering close, one hand braced on the exam table beside my hip.

The tech presses the wand down, adjusting the angle. "There we go," she says casually. The screen flickers as she turns it to us. Shapes form, all blurry but there.

Thump-thump. Thump-thump.

The sound fills the room; it's loud. Mikey freezes, his grip on my hand gets tighter, and I feel his breath hitch beside me.

"That's..." His voice breaks completely this time. He swallows hard, his eyes locked on the screen. "That's... that's a heartbeat."

Kai doesn't speak at all, just sits there staring at the screen as his hands tremble on the table.

"That's ours," Kai finally said. His voice is just above a whisper.

My throat burns from unshed tears threatening to come out.

The tech smiles softly. "Strong heartbeat," she says. "Perfectly normal."

Mikey lets out a breath that sounds kinda like a laugh, then scrubs his hands down his face.

"I... I didn't think it would sound like that," he admits.

"Like what?" I ask.

"Like it's already fighting," he says. "Like it's already here."

Kai leans in closer, his forehead nearly touching mine. "You okay, little dove?" He asks me, but his eyes never leave the screen. Watching the little flickering heartbeat.

I nod. "I think so."

The tech shifts the wand again, frowning slightly, like she is focused.

"Hmm," she hums.

Kai stiffens immediately, and Mikey's head snaps up.

"What?" Mikey asks, quickly.

The tech chuckles at their concern. "Nothing bad, I promise. I just want to adjust something."

Thump-thump.
Thump-thump.

Two rhythms. Not an echo or distortion.

Two.

The room goes completely silent.

Mikey stares at the screen. "Wait," he whispers. "Why–why are there two?

Kai's hand grabs ahold of the table so hard his knuckles turn white.

The tech smiles wider now. "Congratulations," she says gently. "You're having twins."

The words hit me like a shockwave.

"Tw–" Mikey chokes, then laughs in disbelief. "You're joking."

She shakes her head. "Two heartbeats, one sac. Identical twins."

Kai exhales slowly. "Jesus fucking christ," he mutters, dragging his hand down his face.

I start laughing and crying at the same time. My body doesn't know which reaction to choose.

"Two," he breathes out. "There are two of them."

Kai sinks into the chair beside the bed, resting his elbows on his knees, staring at the screen, like it's not real.

Mikey looks up at me with red, tear-filled eyes.

"We're so fucked," He says softly.

Kai snorts, letting the emotions crack his tough exterior. "Yeah, we are."

I look back at the screen again, looking at the two tiny flickering lives, my two little lives that I will protect with everything in me.

The nurse keeps doing things to the computer as we stay there in shock. Measuring something and taking pictures of the babies.

"One more thing." She says, pulling my gaze from the screen. "You seem to be further along than we expected for a first ultrasound, and we can see the gender. Would you like to know?"

I turn and look at Mikey, then to Kai, both of them completely shocked.

"It's up to you, princess." Mikey kisses the top of my head.

"He's right, little dove, the choice isn't ours." Kai agrees.

I look to the nurse and smile, "Can you put it in an envelope for my best friend?"

The nurse smiles at me and nods, grabs the ultrasound pictures, places two in the envelope with a piece of paper, then seals it with a stork sticker.

I grab it from her, and we head out, holding the ultrasounds close to my heart, still not believing the news we got.

Chapter 41

Julia

The next weekend, we are at the ice rink. Mel put together a gender-reveal party for the whole hockey team. Everyone is here to support us.

Mikey and Kai have their skates on, but both wear shirts that say "I'm the dad." I laugh and shake my head because they have been wearing nonstop dad stuff since the appointment.

"Okay, everyone, get on the ice. Mikey and Kai, do you have your sticks?" Mel is in full party-planner mode, barking orders and putting people in their place.

I'm standing at the edge of the ice, not wanting to get on, because I know I will fall and bust my ass.

Mikey and Kai both skate up to me and hold a hand out. I take my first step and slip, but they catch me.

"How do you do this?" I grumble, taking baby steps to get to the center of the ice.

"Baby, we have been skating since we were old enough to walk. Sometimes skating is easier than walking for us." Kai smiles at me before he scoops me up into his arms and skates me to the center of the ice. "Don't you dare drop me!" I smack his chest.

"Baby, I would never drop you." He sets me on my feet, but helps me stay steady.

I turn around and see Mel trying to get on the ice next. As soon as she takes a step on the ice, her feet come out from under her, and Luca is there to catch her fall.

I look up at Mikey and Kai, who both have shit-eating grins on their faces. Because they're thinking the same thing I am. These two are fighting it too hard.

Luca scoops up Mel and sets her in the center of the ice next to me, and she thanks him with a death glare.

"Okay, now that we are all here, and not flat on our asses. Here you go." She pulls out two pucks from her pockets and hands one to each of the twins. One puck has an A on it, and one has a B.

"What are the A and B for?" Kai looks at me, confused.

"To know the difference between the babies. They call them baby A and baby B." I explain.

He looks down at his puck and smiles, "HA, I got baby A!" Kai skates off holding up his stick like he just scored a goal.

"Get your ass back over here, Monroe," Mel barks at him. He comes back and stops fast, spraying snow on her.

"I will get you back for that!" she growls, and Kai just smiles, and the whole team bursts into laughter.

"Okay, assholes, set the pucks down gently, and when you hit them, the color that comes out will be the gender."

Kai and Mikey both set their pucks down,

"Five"

"Four"

"Three"

"Two"

"One"

They both swing, and blue powder explodes from both of them! Mikey and Kai both skate around and scream.

Holy fuck, I am having boys!

My emotions are everywhere; I don't know if I am happy or scared. Probably a lot of both.

Coach skates up to me and smiles, "I hope you know you are fucked. Right?" I smile at him.

"What can I say, coach? *Everything is better in pairs.*" I shrug.

Epilogue

Two years later

"Holy fuck, man, pass him the puck!" Mel is screaming next to me, with Elliot giggling while he is perched on her hip.

Emmett is on my hip, clapping at all the action on the ice.

It's the last period of the Stanley Cup championship game. We are currently tied with the Winnipeg Falcons.

Mikey has been blocking shots like his life depends on it, and Kai, I swear, will have a concussion after how many times he's been checked into the boards.

The crowd is deafening. Every hit makes the glass rattle beneath our hands, and every miss pass pulls groans from the arena. My heart is pounding so hard I can feel it in my throat.

"Daddy fall!" Emmett shouts happily, clapping again as Kai goes down hard near the blue line.

"Buddy, no, daddy is fine," I mutter even though my hands are already sweating.

On the ice, Kai pops right back up as if nothing happened and skates it off. He smacks his stick once on the ground and takes position again. Kai glances over his shoulder at the net, locking eyes with Mikey for a half a second. They don't need words. They never have. It still weirds me out to this day.

"Jesus Christ," Mel mutters. "They're playing line men possessed."

"They always do in the third period," I reply, bounding Emmett slightly when he starts to squirm. "But this is different."

This isn't just any game…This is everything they have poured their heart into, every sacrifice, bruise, and scar.

The Falcons gain control again, streaking down the ice. Mikey drops low, sliding across the crease just in time to block a slap shot that would've gone top shelf. The puck ricochets off his pads and skids wide.

The arena explodes.

"LET'S GO!" Elliot yells, mimicking the crowd with a tiny fist pump. I stare at my son for a long minute. He has curly hair like mine, but blonde like his daddies', and he is wearing a custom-made Vortex jersey with 22/33 on the back. Of course, we had to have both of the boys supporting both of their dads. I also have a custom jersey with the same numbers on it.

"Fuck yes!" Mel yells, bringing my focus back on the game. Kai takes possession, weaving past one defender then another. He fakes left, cuts right, and sends a perfect pass across the ice straight to Luca.

Time slows as Luca winds up and unleashes the shot…

It's like the arena is holding its breath as the puck flies through the air and slams into the back of the net.

Red Lights go off.

Goal horns blaring.

The world detonates.

I scream without realizing it, hugging Emmett so tight that he squeals with laughter. Mel is crying, laughing, and shouting all at once. Elliot nearly launches himself out of her arms.

On the ice, Mikey drops to his knees, head tipped back, chest heaving. Kai is on him a second later, crashing into him, helmets knocking together as the rest of the team piles on Mikey, celebrating the win.

Stanley Cup champions.

My vision blurs as I watch them celebrate. Mikey and Kai both skate over to the glass and hold up their hands. The boys put a hand on theirs, and then they kiss the glass. The whole arena erupts in cheers when I see the big screen showing this moment to the world.

I press a hand to my chest, heart full and aching in the best way.

They made it.

All of us did.

Acknowledgements

I want to start off by saying thank you to all my readers. You guys are absolutely amazing and I wouldn't be here without you.

Next is my family. Thank you to my husband for always watching the kids when I need to hide and write and thank you for always believing in me.

My kids. Thank you for being my biggest cheerleaders. You are the reason I do what I do. You keep me moving forward always.

Next up is my girl Tori. I Don't even know where to start. Without you, this book wouldn't even be done. You had to get onto me more times then I like to count, but shhh we won't mention that. Thank you for always having faith in me and always being willing to dive head first into my books and edit them when ever I ask. Thank you for always being my voice of reason, and helping me navigate my own brain. Without you I swear I would be nothing.

Tasha what do I even say... You have been such a light in my life. You always help me with my books and so much beyond books also. Thank you for willing to fling into my book even though you had a busy schedule. And thank you for always putting a smile on my face when I have been ready to break.

Amanda. Thank you for your positivity. You took a blind chance on me randomly, and I couldn't have asked for a better person to help me along this journey. Between making me giggle with videos of your kiddo and just talking to me when I need to get my thoughts gathered. I appreciate you last minute jumping in to help me.

About the author

Rebekah Lynn is a Navy veteran, a devoted wife, and the mother of two spirited boys who keep life adventurous and full of laughter.

Nestled in the stunning Pacific Northwest, she finds joy in the great outdoors—whether it's hiking rugged trails, camping under the stars, or simply soaking in the beauty of nature with her family.

When she's not chasing boys or braving the elements, Rebekah carves out quiet moments for herself—often with a good book in hand and a heart full of stories waiting to be told. Her writing is infused with honesty, resilience, and a deep appreciation for life's everyday magic.

Rebekah Lynn's social media links!

Also by Rebekah Lynn

She Comes With Me (Book 1)

https://a.co/d/7v9Cnyr

Alex: I never wanted to be in the family business. That's why I joined the Marines. But finding them might have changed my course of action.

Olivia: Being a female cop is not for the faint of heart, nor is being on the gang unit to investigate the Cartel and finding out family secrets that have been kept from me my whole life.

Rachel: I thought I was engaged to the love of my life. Until he was forcing me to leave my home when I had just gotten my dream job and was finally starting to make a name for myself. Now, I have a new relationship that breaks all of my boundaries. But will my past come back and ruin everything?

He Is Ours(Book2)
https://a.co/d/6ADMAeF

Alex: My life was turned upside down by two women who walked into my life unexpectedly. Now one of my girls is being threatened, and I don't take lightly to people threatening what is mine.

Olivia: I was held captive by the Drug Lord, and now that I am free, my trust is being tested more than I expected.

Rachel: My past is coming back for revenge, and little do they know, I am not the scared girl I was before. I have people who love me, but will that be enough?

They Belong To Me(Book 3)
https://a.co/d/3JI4wOu

Alex: An interruption during my wedding sends everything spiraling. All I wanted was one day of peace, one day where my family could breathe. My grandfather has resurfaced from the dark holes he has been hiding in and is out to destroy everything I've built. I'll burn the world before I let that happen.

Olivia: Pregnant or not, I'm not standing on the sidelines. I'm still haunted by the man who took me, still fighting the fear that he'll come back for me. But this time, I'm not running. I'll protect my baby and my family, even if it means facing the darkness I swore I'd never touch again.

Rachel: My wife is carrying our future. My husband's being hunted. And I've finally unleashed the demon inside me. I've spent years keeping it caged, but love and fear have a way of snapping chains. Whoever comes for us will learn our love may be twisted, but it's lethal.

The Monster Within

(Blood On The Apple Prequel)

https://a.co/d/3Hh7Dtg

When I was 14 years old, my life changed forever. I realized I was becoming the monster I had feared my whole life. Now I am the monster walking through plain sight.

Made in United States
Troutdale, OR
01/30/2026

46394097R00130